**CHIUN WATCHED HER FROM HIS PERCH
ON THE TREE.**

The mysterious pain in his side would not fade.
And he could not help but be affected by the
performance of the Priestess. He was, after all,
only a human being—and this night, he felt
more human than he had in decades.

"A Master of Sinanju never fails to be man
enough for any woman," the Priestess chided
him. "And you are not so very old. And this body
is ready for you."

Her glistening flesh reflected the firelight. With
hundreds of worshippers gathered there, it was
still as if they were alone, Chiun and the Holy
Mother.

It was in this moment of distraction and
temptation, when Chiun was allowing himself
to wallow in the weakness of his humanity, that
another acolyte struck at him.

"Old fool!" Chiun cursed in his mind as the trees
exploded around him and something like an iron
fist engulfed his body and Chiun felt himself
rocketed into the skies.

CREATED BY WARREN MURPHY & RICHARD SAPIR

THE DESTROYER

HOLY MOTHER

A GOLD EAGLE BOOK FROM

WORLDWIDE®

TORONTO • NEW YORK • LONDON
AMSTERDAM • PARIS • SYDNEY • HAMBURG
STOCKHOLM • ATHENS • TOKYO • MILAN
MADRID • WARSAW • BUDAPEST • AUCKLAND

First edition July 2006

ISBN-13: 978-0-373-63259-6
ISBN-10:   0-373-63259-2

Special thanks and acknowledgment to Tim Somheil
for his contribution to this work.

HOLY MOTHER

Printed in U.S.A.

And for the Glorious House of Sinanju,
at www.warrenmurphy.com

1

It was funny how mass murder could put the brakes on a thriving tourism trade. The bottom fell out of the Union Island jerk-chicken industry in a big way. Cart-pusher Jerome Churchill Hanger watched his business prospects crumble, along with the local economy.

Everything had been going gangbusters for a couple of years, with tens of thousands of visitors coming to the island. Resorts were built. The one and only town on the island was given the full quaint treatment: cobblestone street paving, brand-new, antique-looking streetlamps, a fresh updating of old-fashioned building facades. It all looked so inviting in the travel brochures and on Web sites.

But those improvements made the contrast more alarming when the photos of bloody corpses were broadcast on the global news stations.

Jerry Hanger the jerk-chicken seller didn't know what the killing was about, exactly. It wasn't the islanders' affair. The victims—and there were lots of them—were almost exclusively visitors and recent transplants to the island. It was too bad, all the killing, but the islanders were keeping their distance from the whole affair. It felt safer that way.

Jerry's auntie whispered that the killings were caused by evil people who had come to Union Island during the recent boom years, bringing with them the devils that possessed them. Jerry Hanger was a modern man and he didn't buy into his auntie's superstitions and he sure didn't believe in people getting possessed by devils.

But he was satisfied with keeping his nose out of the killing business. Let the mainland feds and the island officials handle it, then pack up their bodies and go home.

Only forty-eight hours after the killings had commenced, and already the island was emptying out. The tourists couldn't flee fast enough. The bodies went soon after that. Then the mainland officials. And today, many of the recent transplants started pulling up their shallow roots and departing.

Paradise hadn't panned out.

JERRY HANGER'S jerk-chicken sales to the visitors dropped to almost nothing, so all he could do was bring his prices back down to pretourism levels and steer the cart back into the islander neighborhoods.

It felt good, like going home again, and the old calm was settling over the island. He found himself enjoying his job more than he had in years. He liked selling to his people, the locals. They knew good jerk chicken when they tasted it. They didn't treat him like a novelty item, the way the visitors did.

The only downside to the whole affair, as far as Jerry was concerned, was the disappearance of the island president. On the night of the mayhem the president was airlifted off the island to safety. Everyone who cared about the well-being of the president breathed a sigh of relief. So long as he was safe from harm, then everything else would work itself out.

But when the killing was done and the bodies were being counted, there was the devastating news that the president had vanished right out of the helicopter that was carrying him to safety. No one could understand it.

Initially the death of the president consumed the islanders. They were heartbroken, even traumatized. The mass murder in their streets and the disruption to their economic infrastructure were minor compared to the heartache of the president's death.

But by the end of the first day everybody Jerry Hanger knew seemed to be changing their tune on the president. What had been so great about that guy, after all? What had they liked about him? He was just another transplant from the mainland. Maybe it wasn't so bad that he was gone.

It was a shame about Minister Summens, though. She had been the symbol of all that was beautiful about Union Island. She was the spokesperson and public face for the island, and it was a very pretty face indeed. And a nice body, too. She had been the only tourism official on any Caribbean island who actually appeared in commercials as her own bikini model. She was a shot in the arm for Union Island's self-esteem.

And now she was dead. Too bad.

As the dusk sky became bloodred, Jerry realized he was just outside the cemetery. There was no living soul in sight, but he wasn't alone. Nearby were the outlines in the sandy soil where the fresh graves were dug, to bury the handful of locals who had been caught up in the mayhem.

Dawn Summens was there. No family to be sent home to on the mainland, so they had just buried her here.

What amazed Jerry was the quiet that had descended now that the visitors were gone. He heard the breeze for the first time in years. He could hear the cry of gulls on the beach, and the beach was half a mile away. He could hear—what?

What was it he was hearing? Was it the island itself? Had there always been this thrumming undercurrent that seemed to emit from the very soil? Was it something that he had been used to, in the time before the bloody tourists, coming back now that the tourists were history? What *was* that sound?

Though Jerry Hanger was a modern man, who didn't believe in the foolish old traditions of his auntie, he could have sworn he was hearing some sort of a sound coming from the line of freshly dug graves near the street side of the fence.

The dusk was coming down fast and hard, and in minutes it would be black in the secluded cemetery. Jerry Hanger thrust his cart rapidly up the road to the comfort of the islander's shanty village. He said nothing, not even to his auntie.

After years of scoffing her superstitions, how could he now admit to her that he had heard the whispers of the restless dead?

SHE CAME TO AWARENESS in the middle of a scream and realized she had been screaming for a long time.

She had become paralyzed some time ago from carelessly touching the dried remains of a sea creature stolen from the island's natural history museum, forgetting to use rubber gloves. Without protection, the simple act of touching the specimen allowed its peculiar toxins to seep into her body through her skin. The dosage was enough to leave her paralyzed but aware.

She could hear and she could feel it when living hands touched her flesh to drag her from her stalled car. Her eyes popped open at one point and she could see perfectly. She watched the doctor perform a cursory examination of her limp body. She felt the touch of his cold steel stethoscope. He pressed it to her chest, listened for a beating heart—but not for long—then shook his head and walked away.

Why had he not heard her heart beating? He was careless. She knew her heart was working. She could feel it. Slowly, to be sure, but she knew she was alive.

Surely the doctor would have more tests to perform on her before he made his declaration of her death.

She was just one in the long lineup of victims, now laid out on the floor of the very museum from which she had stolen the specimen that poisoned her. All the victims were dead. The doctor went through them as if conducting tests on an assembly line. Then he laid out the death certificates on a reading table and filled them in methodically with a ballpoint.

She was just one more corpse to be certified— even though she was still alive.

Once she was officially and legally deceased, she was zipped into a plastic bag and put in a truck.

Many of the dead were taken to the airport for transport back to the mainland United States. She wondered where they would take her. Her hometown? There was no one to claim her there. She was one of a few bodies that remained on the island after the airlift of corpses.

As the truck moved on to its next stop, she was frantically trying to get her body to respond. She had to communicate with her handlers. She had to do something. *Anything.*

She was put in the official, tiny Union Island morgue. She could tell by the closeness of the air and the bone-chilling cold that she was in a refrigerated drawer. She couldn't even shiver. The cold seemed to go on forever, and she finally lost awareness.

She came to when her body was moving.

She was still inside her body bag, but her eyes must have popped open again. As she felt herself wheeled over a threshold, she could see the blaze of the warming sun glow through the black plastic of her body bag.

The warmth felt wonderful, but she knew where she was going now. To her burial. She was lifted off the gurney and she felt strong hands on her legs and shoulders. She struggled to make herself move or make some small sound, offer some signal that she was alive.

Her eyes were working again! She was blinking!

In a moment, she felt herself lifted up and lowered again, into another tight space. The surfaces at her sides were padded. She was in her coffin.

Wait a second—she was still in the body bag. They had to take her out of the bag. They would have to take her out to embalm her, right?

But they didn't. They were scared to touch her. She might be toxic. They were going to leave her sealed up. She was like a piece of moldy meat found in the back of the fridge in a sandwich bag. Why open it before tossing it in the trash?

The coffin was placed in the hearse. It drove across the island in mere minutes—the island was not a big place. Soon she felt the shushing of the tires on sand and she knew she was on the unfinished back road from the town into the unpopular, non-beachfront, Union Island interior. The road went to the huddle of shanties and huts that housed the islanders, and along the way the unpaved trail curved by Union Island's only cemetery.

That's where she was taken. That's where they laughed and made jokes and in minutes had wrapped her box in ropes and lowered her into the hole.

What about a service? A prayer? A few kind words? Didn't *anybody* even come to say goodbye?

She felt the thump as the box settled into position, followed by the horrible lack of movement. She heard the shower of sandy soil over the coffin lid and the sound became muted as the inches of soil grew. Then there was no sound at all.

She tried to make her own sound. She tried to scream. For hours and hours she tried but the scream would not come. She opened and closed her eyes in the blackness, but there was nothing to see

How long would the air last? Not long. The box was small.

Finally, sensing that it was night, she dropped off to sleep, hoping that while she was sleeping the air would finally give out. It would be a blessing to never awaken.

Somehow she had awakened. Her body was working again. She had started screaming. Her body was capable of movement again. Later, she found she could lift her hands, and she weakly felt around the inside of her box, which told her how precious little room there was. Terror brought her strength back and she scratched through the plastic bag and pounded at the inside of the coffin, knowing all along it would do her no good.

She was an intelligent, well-educated woman,

and the rational part of her mind wondered why she had not died of suffocation. She must have been in this box for a day, buried in the earth, and no matter how porous the island soil, it couldn't let in enough air to replenish the confines of the coffin. So how was she finding enough air to breathe?

Why couldn't she just die?

Once, when she stopped screaming from exhaustion, she felt the faintest touch of cool air on her hand. Her nugget of rational thinking latched on to the fact, then dismissed it as fantasy. There was no way fresh air could reach a buried coffin.

But the feather touch of cool air became unmistakable. The oxygen that had been trapped in the box must have been used up. So new air was reaching her. But how?

She began to work with her hands on the walls of the box. She ripped off the padding and tapped the wood. There was something different here. The sound of her tapping was less solid.

She worked at the wood hour after hour, until her fingers were raw. Finally she loosened a shard of wood and worked it tirelessly until she pulled it off. She heard the screeching of the nails and she felt sand sift through the opening.

But not much sand.

She thrust her hand through the opening and felt

what lay beyond. It was an open space in the earth. She didn't know how to explain its existence and she didn't care at the moment. It was there, and so far it was keeping her alive.

She tore at the edges of the opening in her coffin.

Soon she found she had opened a corridor into which her entire arm would fit, and she explored the open space by touch. It was an adjoining grave. It was many years old, judging from the shriveled, desiccated feel of the remains. There were at least three bodies, bones as dry as corn husks. Her groping hands discovered that their own coffins were reduced to damp droppings of wood powder and fragments of corroded nails.

Above the coffins was a concrete roof. It was designed to hold the dead in their place in the event the island was inundated by a storm surge—something that happened three or four times each century here in the Caribbean hurricane zone. When the ocean soaked into the sandy soil, the coffins of the recently dead became boats that rose up through the earth. There was nothing quite so disturbing as seeing the burial box of a recently deceased family member floating down the flooded streets.

She realized she had been buried close to the burial plot of one of the wealthier island families. Their coffins were old and disintegrated and the bodies had long since rotted away. There was hardly any smell as they waited the passage of time in their little hollow place.

She once ran things around here. She knew what a pauper's grave on Union Island entailed. She even knew how much it cost the government coffers to buy the cheap coffin she had been buried in. She was in a cheap box in a cheap grave. No concrete cap in her plot. Just five or six feet of loose island soil, made light by silica sand and crushed coral.

She could get out of that.

She laughed at her own madness. Once she had been buried up to her neck in sand on the beach in Jamaica by an old boyfriend, and she could barely move. There was no way to get through six feet of it.

But she had to do something. Better to die struggling than to lie here until the end came. She was not the kind to be passive. She hadn't experienced her many successes in life by being passive. She had fought for her position as tourism minister of Union Island. She had come close to being president and had come close to gaining the island its independence and had come close to being very powerful and wealthy. She was a fighter and she would fight now.

She folded her body until her legs were under her

and her back was lodged against the coffin lid. Even her slim, lithe body was compressed painfully. She pushed upward and felt the wood crack. The wood was cheap. She felt the shards tear her back flesh, but she didn't feel the pain.

The top of the coffin cracked into pieces and the sand cascaded in around her. She forced her body up and into the sand-fall and thrust her arm up to her chest. She spread her hands in front of her, trying to make a hollow to trap a precious pint of air. It was what they told you to do if you were being buried in an avalanche of snow. It didn't work well with free-flowing sand, but the adhesive nature of the soil mixed with the sand gave it just enough stickiness to let her create a pocket of air. She had one or two more breaths.

But she was on her feet. Her head was that much closer to the surface. For a moment she allowed herself to feel optimistic—only to feel the weight of the sand entrap her lower body as it was enveloped in soil. The coffin, where she had been lying in a chamber of air a moment ago, was now filled up. No air pocket left below her. As if she could have retreated to that place anyway.

She could move her legs. The air in her little space grew unbreathable in just seconds, and so she screamed into the little space. If there was a rational part of her mind still operating, it would have known that screaming was an inefficient use of the precious little oxygen her body retained in its cells, but she ignored rational thought. She was as good as dead. Dead. Might as well go out screaming.

Then something happened. Maybe it was a burst of adrenaline or maybe some survival instinct kicked in, but it felt like an electric shock jolting her body. It had an element of sound, like someone shouting in a speaker right next to her ear. It actually startled her.

She stopped screaming and her fear escalated. It was a new kind of a fear—a fear of what was in the earth with her. Not dead bodies. Not her bony neighbors in the adjoining burial plot, but something else more terrifying than death. Her muscles forced her limbs to work with surprising force. Strength born of terror brought her higher up in her crouch, and she was surprised to realize that her position had shifted her posture. During her thrashing, she had managed to straighten her legs under her. She was in fact worming her way out through the soil, moving closer to the surface.

But her air pocket was gone. She had taken her last breath. She either made it to the surface with what she had or she never made it to the surface. She pushed, moving her hands mere inches through the soil. She was slowing down.

She felt the shock again and heard the startling sound and her body recoiled toward the surface. She could stand dying in a cocoon of earth but she couldn't stand the horror of the thing that was here in the earth with her.

But she was weakening. The final surge of adrenaline was used up. Her energy was depleted and her vision filled with sickly images that she knew meant her mind was being starved of oxygen. The shocking disturbances continued to come, but her depleted mind could no longer react. As her mind shut down, she imagined that the shocking sounds had taken on the aspect of human speech.

Worm, the voice said. *Be a worm in the soil. You are capable of that at the least. Are you at least a worm?*

She was being humiliated. Her tormentor was adding insult to horror. But she was seconds away from death and even her terror of the thing in the earth was fading. Whatever was tormenting her, it would go away soon. Everything would go away soon.

Then she imagined in the soil was moving around her, and that something was forcing its way through the earth from below, and then she tasted the stale underground air. Corpse air, she was breathing. And a hollow place had formed again between herself and the chamber of the desiccated bones. She felt something vile and tubular and segmented scrounging in the dirt and scraping against her flesh, crawling on her with a thousand tiny legs. She gagged on the air—but it was air and she could breathe it.

But it was so repulsive she tried to push the thing away, only to find that the segmented worm-thing had encircled both wrists and begun to wriggle with them up through the soil. It dragged her wrists with it until her arms were being torn from their sockets. Her bones were being stretched beyond their capacity. She moved her legs as best she could to free the soil around them, easing the stretching of her backbone while she fought to dislodge the terrible thing.

Then she felt a new sensation when one hand was suddenly free of the dirt. The other hand followed it. The worm had pulled her hands out of the grave and into the world above. If she could only get her head above the earth, then she could get free of the disgusting worm that opened its orifice at her mouth and regurgitated corpse air into her throat. Being free of the thing in the grave was more important than saving her life.

With her hands free, she had new leverage, and she pulled her body through the loose soil. She pushed with her impossibly buried feet, and her flesh scraped and wriggled through the dirt until somehow her head broke free.

The moonlight blinded her.

She flung her head from side to side. She retched on clean air. Only when she stopped choking did she realize that whatever had been attached to her face was gone. She was sucking in clean air, and maybe the worm had been nothing but a nightmare.

But there was still the nightmare of her real situation. She was still chest-deep in her grave.

She clawed at the earth for another eternity, stopping to rest again and again. There wasn't as much urgency now. She was alive. When her eyes were finally accustomed to the light, she saw the old headstone of the adjoining grave. It was the Colkan family plot. The bones she had handled so intimately were those of Rodney and Melinda Colkan, husband and wife, both dead in the sixties and in the grave for half again as many years. Enith Colkan, mother of Rodney, was in there with them. A cozy little family resting place, but how did Melinda feel about the arrangement?

During her rests, she wondered what the long-gone Colkans had been like. She thought of them with a kind of affection. They had, after all, saved her life.

But something else had been down there, as well,

and it had not been as amiable as the Colkans. What was it?

Maybe just her imagination. All she knew was that she was alive now, and that she was not the same person she had once been. Something was gone. She had left part of herself in the grave. Something that normal people have, she no longer had.

Call it sanity. Call it reason. Call it what you want—she no longer had use for it.

She was thought to be dead. How could she use that to her advantage? She was already thinking about her next step, even before she had managed to get her knees free of the grave.

When she finally stood, she felt surprisingly strong and fit, and she turned to leave the cemetery. The fence was not much challenge for one who had just clawed her way out of the grave.

When she reached the road, she looked one way and then the other. One way led to the little town that used to be her home. That was days ago, when she was a bureaucrat in the Union Island government. It was a town of gift shops, restaurants and beach homes belonging to wealthy Americans.

Take the road the other way, and you came to the village of the islanders. It was a place of ramshackle shacks and little frame houses on cracked concrete slabs.

She walked to the islanders' village.

It was quiet and dark. She didn't know the time, but there was no sign of dawn. When she came to the village she headed for the first house.

It was, in fact, home of Jerry the jerk-chicken merchant, where he lived with his auntie, his mother, his sister and his sister's children.

She didn't bother to knock, but pushed through the screen door and headed for the kitchenette. All she cared about was getting water. She wondered how long it had been since she'd had water.

It was warm, gritty water, but she slurped handfuls of it before she became aware of the disturbance she was causing in the home. They thought there was an intruder. When the lights came on, the household got a look at her and they thought something different.

She was filthy, bloody, ghastly. Her clothing had disintegrated until only a mass of rags hung about her waist. Her hands were torn and dangled shreds of her flesh, and beneath the muck she was pale as a corpse. Her rich dark hair was matted around her shoulders.

Jerry Hanger knew who she was. He knew what she was—something his auntie had always warned him about. He had never heeded to her devil talk.

He wanted to run, but he couldn't move until she

laughed at him, and that was all his mind could take. He fled, howling.

When she was alone in the hut, she rummaged for food in the little refrigerator. She found nothing but a loaf of spongy white bread. But there was a delicious smell coming from somewhere.

She found the smell coming from the cart at the back of house. Inside was a plastic bag of chicken parts, already lathered with spices. Jerry Hanger's famous jerk chicken. Raw, but she didn't care. She wolfed it down, tearing the flesh off the bone with her flashing white teeth.

There was noise out front, so she left through the rear and circled back to the road, her thirst and hunger temporarily quenched. She started thinking in more practical terms as she loped into the main town.

There was a guard around the darkened government house, but she slipped past easily enough and found one of her hidden keys, and went inside. The place was being inventoried, apparently. And her belongings were in boxes.

The former island president was out of the picture. She found a newspaper that was dated to the day after everything had gone wrong. The president was assumed dead. Jumped out of a rescue helicopter.

She considered that. She had known the president intimately. He was a fantastic coward. He would never have killed himself. Somebody had killed him.

Strangely enough, she somehow knew who had done the deed.

"Remo," she said out loud.

She found the belongings she needed, and changes of clothing, and took all the mad money that was stashed in the place. It was amazing how little she needed to move on to the next phase of her life.

"Remo," she said.

She knew the one named Remo. They'd had lunch together. He was important. She wasn't sure how or why. "Remo."

Her new life. "Remo."

She didn't know what it meant, but there was no doubt. Remo was her new life—whatever that meant.

She didn't know anything else about him. How to find him. What to do when she found him.

She would see to it that he found her.

"Remo."

The word kept popping out of her mouth. She ought to be keeping it shut until she was off the island, at least.

How was she going to get off the island without attracting attention? Was there anybody left on this miserable sand pile that might help smuggle her away?

Maybe there was.

2

His name was Remo and he was on his way to assassinate his first dairy mogul.

First he had to get past the dairy mogul's private army. Remo had taken on private armies before, though not armies outfitted in white jumpsuits with white bow ties and paper hats.

His mind tripped over the incongruities of the grunt who emerged from the underbrush a few miles ahead, all in white. He was a fully equipped military grunt: sunglasses, scowl and an automatic rifle, and he held them all perfectly poised as Remo approached. Remo slowed the rental SUV to a crawl, and the grunt began to struggle to maintain the perfect expression of deep seriousness. He gave up and relaxed his bunched-up forehead, and concentrated on holding his head in exactly the right position to reflect a beam of piercing sunlight in Remo's face.

Remo spent half his life dealing with petty power

mongers and they irritated him to no end. He reached to the floor mats of the rental car and felt around until he had two grains of sand that had been tracked in. Remo put one between his left thumb and finger, stuck it out the window and flicked it.

The grain of sand traveled at the speed of a subsonic bullet until it crashed into the left hinge of the sunglasses. The hinge shattered and the sunglasses swung across the grunt's face like a pendulum on its remaining arm. The grunt yanked them off, stared at the damage, failed to understand the cause, but then shoved them back on his face in a hurry, valiantly trying to regain his composure. The sunglasses balanced precariously on the nose bridge and one arm until Remo flicked the second grain of sand. The right hinge shattered. The grunt rolled his eyes to the ground, but kept his head held high. The sunglasses, miraculously, stayed on the grunt's nose as Remo rolled to a stop.

"I get it," Remo said. "You're a milkman!"

The grunt ignored the comment, but the stiffening of his facial muscles told Remo that he was humiliated by the outfit.

"Nice glasses," Remo added. "Is that the new style? My granny had some like that. Never could figure out how she kept them from falling off."

"Your business?"

"Assassination, occasionally, but there's a lot of busywork in between real jobs. What's your line of work? Are you a milkman-mercenary or a mercenary-milkman?"

"You have ID?"

"Yes."

"Show me."

"You first."

"Sir, you will present your ID or you will be arrested."

"I'm pretty sure I don't have to give you my ID until you give me yours."

"Sir, this is private property and state law does give property owners the right to defend their property. Which I will not fail to do unless you identify yourself at once."

"You must have spent hours memorizing that bowl of bulldookey. The fact is, this is public state property to the top of the ridge, which I think means you've got weapons on state land and that's a felony and so maybe you'd better give me your ID first."

The milkman grunt made a sound of deep and condescending exasperation and felt for his pseudo-military ID badge, tucked in his pants' pocket and attached with a retractable tether to his belt. He pulled out the badge wallet without losing the armless sunglasses teetering on the bridge of his nose, so he never saw Remo flick another grain of sand. The grunt yelped and dropped the badge, then patted his belt and his pocket.

"It fell on the ground," Remo said.

The grunt spotted the wallet on the dusty earth, trailing a neatly severed cord. The grunt frowned and bent, keeping his head high, committed to keeping the sunglasses over his eyes no matter what. He felt around his feet for the wallet, and Remo flicked another grain of sand. The wallet flopped away.

"You want some help?" he offered.

"Stay in the car, civilian!"

"Sure thing." Remo found more sand on the floor mats and was pleased when he made the grunt lose the sunglasses during a graceless lunge for the wildly escaping ID wallet.

Finally he tackled the wallet, clutched it to his chest and leaped to his feet, waving a hand in the air in search of the piece of fishing line that must have been used to perpetrate the prank. He glared at the scrubby terrain where the prankster must be hiding. By the time he returned to the car he was in a foul mood and thrust the wallet at Remo.

"Good enough for you?"

"Sergeant Ready," Remo said, "you need better sunblock." He removed the visor and displayed the mirror for the grunt, all red face and huge, clownlike white eyes. "And look at your pantsuit. It's a mess."

"It's not a pantsuit."

"My granny used to wear outfits just like that. She called them pantsuits. Hers didn't have an embroidered cow on the pocket."

"Your ID!" Ready snapped.

Remo gave him his wallet.

"Penultimate?"

"Yes."

"Remo Penultimate?"

"Yes."

"Sounds fake."

"Do you give everybody this much attitude when they come through here?" Remo asked. "I've met lots of lowlifes drunk on their own crumb of authority, but you're one of the most obnoxious ever."

Sergeant Ready thrust out his lower jaw. He was not a milkman to be trifled with, and his patience would only extend so far. Remo Penultimate had pushed him too far. "Sir, please step out of the car."

"No, thanks."

Now, you never said no to Sergeant Ready when he asked you to step out of the car. Never. He snatched the rifle off his back and leveled it at the driver of the SUV. "Get out of the car! Now!"

"What happened to your gun?" Remo asked. Although Sergeant Ready had followed his training and taken his aggressive posture several arm's lengths from the vehicle, the driver somehow stretched out and grasped the muzzle of the automatic rifle, and it was all so quick that Ready didn't have time to react.

"See?" Remo said. "It's all bent."

Ready stared at the muzzle. It was pinched flat and twisted like a soda straw.

"This is an act, isn't it?" Remo said. "I mean, the milkman clothes and the thing with the glasses falling off and the ID that goes flipping around and the funny gun? You're some sort of a roadside entertainer, right?"

"Sir. Get out of the car. Now." Sergeant Ready unholstered his sidearm.

Remo got out of the SUV so fast that Sergeant Ready couldn't follow the action, until the man was standing directly in front of him. It happened in an eye blink.

"I thought so. Another prop." Remo was holding Ready's sidearm—and showing him how the butt could be twisted back and forth as if it were made of rubber.

Sergeant Ready screeched, grabbed the gun and felt the butt himself—solid steel, but now hopelessly mangled. He slammed it into the ground.

"You've got passion, I'll give you that, but the slapstick act needs work," Remo said.

Sergeant Ready yanked out the handcuffs and snapped them on Remo Penultimate's right wrist— only to find he had somehow shackled his own left wrist instead. He grabbed Remo's left wrist, then found himself landing on the ground on his back, and there was some movement he couldn't follow. When it was all over, his left ankle was in the other loop of the handcuffs, which were stretched taut between his legs.

"Well, it's kind of funny, I suppose," Remo Penultimate said doubtfully. "Here you go." He tossed a quarter in the dirt alongside Ready. "I'd love to stay and see more, but I've got a meeting with Mr. Milque."

Remo got in his SUV and drove up the road.

Sergeant Ready struggled desperately to his feet and grabbed his holstered radio. Smashed. He ended up skipping down the hill with his upper body bent low over his ankle. If he let an intruder get past his checkpoint without at least warning the main house, he was a dead man. Stan Milque did not like surprises. That was why he had armed guards in the first place.

There was a spare radio in the camouflaged hut that served as his guard post. He got the main house on the line and warned of an intruder.

Base was not amused by his failure. "You let one man get past you, Ready? How'd you manage that?"

Ready wasn't sure what had happened. Everything had just seemed to go catastrophically wrong. "Sabotage!" he blurted.

"Sabotage?" The shift commander wasn't buying it.

"You want me to explain it now?" Ready snapped. "Intruder ETA is one minute."

"We'll handle it." The radio went dead. Ready was relieved that he would have time to come up with some sort of an explanation for what happened—if only he could figure it out himself.

STAN MILQUE FIDGETED at the window and paced the floor of his private office. There had been an intruder warning—and then nothing for many long minutes. He watched the white-uniformed men covering the entire grounds once each minute, finding nothing.

"Is Milque really your last name?" Remo asked.

Stan Milque spun around and found himself facing a stranger. "You're the intruder."

"Brains like that are what make you a dairy mogul."

"How did you get past my men?"

"The Milky Militia? Piece of cake."

Stan Milque backed behind the desk and used his foot to nudge the button on the silent alarm on the desk leg.

"Who are you?" Milque asked.

"Remo. Something or other."

"Penultimate."

Remo snapped his fingers. "That's it. You've been talking to Sergeant Unprepared."

"Is that your real name?"

"Nah. I don't even know what penultimate means. But the name doesn't matter. It's the purpose of my visit."

"Which is?"

"Kill you, put an end to your reign of dairy terror, et cetera. It's the same old shtick, but each job is satisfying in its own way."

Milque nodded. "I see."

"You do?"

"Absolutely." At that moment Milque grabbed for the combat shotgun in its quick-release harness mounted under the surface of the desk, even as the double doors of the private office flew open. Armed military men burst inside, their weapons aimed at the chest of Remo Penultimate.

"Get on the ground, scumbag!" barked the commander. He was wearing a sweat-stained white jumpsuit, but his paper hat was lost somewhere.

"Have at him, boys," Remo announced, and waved at Stan Milque.

"I'm talking to *you,* asshole!" The commander got in Remo's face, grabbed Remo's wrist and jerked it behind his back.

Remo had extraordinarily thick wrists. He took his wrist back and took the weapons away from the commander and the other milkmen, tossing them into the ceiling. The weapons were buried deep in the textured plaster, their protruding halves thrumming like taut wire. Remo herded the milkmen back the way they had come, using a series of quick, bone-breaking shoves and jostles. Finally he snatched the commander off his feet, turned him sideways and flung him into the rest of the commandos. Every milkman went down.

"I should take up bowling," Remo commented, slamming the door.

Stan Milque triggered the combat shotgun. He was a few feet away from Remo Penultimate, and Remo should have ended up dead on the floor with his clothes and flesh shredded.

Remo did seem to make a quick movement in the direction of the floor, but it was in the instant before the air filled with screaming buckshot. Then the walls were ruined and Remo was back where he had been as if nothing had happened. There wasn't a scratch on him. Remo lifted the shotgun out of Milque's hands and flung it underhanded at the door. The door was just bursting open and the flying shotgun skewered three of the four men who were entering.

Milky Commando Four did a commendable job of keeping his cool as his comrades expired noisily at his feet.

"Hands up!"

"No, thanks."

His rifle fired into Remo Penultimate's chest.

Remo did something impossible—he sensed the trajectory of the approaching rounds and moved himself somewhere else, and he did it fast enough to actually avoid being struck by the bullets.

The rounds slammed through one of the picture windows behind Stan Milque, and Milque hit the deck.

The gunman kept firing at Remo, who did a kind of gliding dance around the office that kept himself and the bullets from ever being in the same place at the same time, and every step brought him closer to the gunman. Remo lifted the gun away and sent it deep into the ceiling, which now resembled an upside-down firearms forest.

Stan Milque heard the gunfire stop, heard the crunch of the weapon entering the plaster and then he heard another crunch. This was a different kind of a crunch.

When he looked fearfully over the top of the desk, he saw that the final gunman had been embedded in the ceiling along with the firearms. Unlike the weapons, the gunman dripped.

"Anybody else?" Remo Penultimate called out the office door.

There was no answer.

"Finally." Remo hauled Stan Milque off the floor and hooked Milque's sport jacket on an old-fashioned iron chandelier in the middle of the room. Stan Milque felt pain where the jacket cut off the circulation to his shoulders, but he wasn't about to complain about it.

"Okay, tell me what you did wrong," Remo demanded.

"What?"

"You're a bad man. I know you are. I just don't know what kind of badness you do. I don't think your crimes end at silly uniforms for the hired help."

Stan Milque was desperate to understand what Remo was talking about.

Remo explained. "See, I'm a peon. The low man on the totem pole. I get told what to do and I go do it. Smith says—Smith is my boss-man—he says, 'Remo, go kill Mr. So-and-So.' And I say, 'Sure thing, boss!' And I go kill Mr. So-and-So. But usually I know why Mr. So-and-So is being killed. Maybe he bombed a building, maybe he shot some innocent bystanders in a bank heist, whatever. The point is, I know why. See?"

What Stan Milque was seeing at the moment was his hired mercenary—the one who had been thrust hip deep in the ceiling. His body weight was slowly dragging him out of the hole, but the shattered beams and shards of plaster were trying to hang on to him. It was making a mess of the already messed-up mercenary. The dripping blood became a trickle.

"So Smith says, 'Go get the Milque Man right away, Remo!' and I say, 'Sure thing, Mr. Smith! I'm on it!' And here I am. So I took care of the Milky Military and now I'm gonna take care of the Milky Man himself, but now we come back to the question of job satisfaction. See, for me to be really fulfilled in my job, I have to know the reason. So, Milque, what's the reason?"

"No reason! I swear!" He was rotating slowly on the chandelier and the madman Remo Penultimate was coming back into his field of vision.

Remo clearly didn't believe Stan Milque.

"You and I both know there is a reason."

"There isn't!"

Remo made a long-distance phone call on Stan

Milque's private phone, without asking permission. He dialed information and asked for the number of the Scranton, California, U-Pull-It Auto Parts.

Stan Milque was more confused than ever.

"Hi, sweetheart. Don't pretend. I know it's you. Fine. I need a block from a 1973 Ford Maverick. A 302, 4-cylinder. Got one? Oh, hi, Smitty."

Stan Milque heard every word, and his mind reeled.

"I'm here with my friend Stan Milque. No, not yet. I want to know what he did first. Because, to hear him tell it, he's an innocent man. I'm not going to assassinate an innocent man. I want to know the truth. What did he do?"

Stan Milque knew he was in the hands of a lunatic, but a deadly lunatic. He had now rotated back on the cadaver lodged in the ceiling.

"Really?" Remo was saying. "You don't say? I'm appalled."

Remo hung up.

"Smith tells me you're a very bad man," Remo announced. "He says to me, 'Remo, that Stan Milque tried to get a whole school district hooked on amphetamines!' I couldn't believe it. 'Put meth in the milk.' Is this true?"

"No!" Stan Milque said.

Remo came close and placed Milque's elbow between his thumb and finger, and he pinched. Milque stuttered from the pain.

"It was just a *little* meth! It wouldn't have killed them!"

"That's a bad, bad thing to do. Luckily, my boss was keeping an eye on you. Says the locals couldn't seem to make the connection between the drug traffic in this county and the local dairy mogul, but he did, and when he caught wind of your new scheme, he knew it was time to send in his gopher in a big hurry."

"It was a business decision! I needed to expand my customer base! You know how much money I make? I got lots of money! You want lots of money?"

"Got lots," Remo said. "So I'm told. But mostly, I got job satisfaction!"

"No!"

"Yes."

Remo did his job, and left another cadaver dripping on the carpet in the private office.

As he left the silent country home, he rifled the wallet he had taken from his victim. "I knew it," he muttered when he found the driver's license with the name Stan Munstein. "I knew it wasn't really Milque."

Remo's last name wasn't really Penultimate, either. Once, his last name was Williams. But that was in another lifetime.

Once, he has been a combat soldier fighting in foreign wars. Then he was a beat cop in Jersey. Then he was a convicted murderer who sizzled in the electric chair. Then he was a nobody—just another headstone in the graveyard. Dead and buried.

But he wasn't really dead. He woke from the electrocution with a bad headache and a lousy job offer: be an assassin for a clandestine agency of the U.S. government called CURE. He didn't want the job, but the alternative was to be assassinated himself.

Remo Williams took the job, and excelled as an assassin. The job had its ups and its downs, but sometimes Remo experienced true job satisfaction—such as when he made some horrible person go away forever. Like Stan Milque. The son of a bitch was selling crystal meth to twelve-year-olds, and when business slowed down, he came up with a way to create a bunch of new customers in a big hurry. Dose the lunchroom milk supply.

The thing was, it only took a single dose of crystal meth to create an addict.

Remo didn't want to picture the result. The ruined lives. The agony of the families. Inevitably, a slew of new, young addicts who would do anything to get another meth fix.

When he got back to his hidden SUV, he didn't feel fulfilled any longer. He felt emotionally ill. He'd stopped Stan Milque before the scheme was accomplished, but who would stop the next guy who tried it? And the next? And the next?

Out in the road was the mercenary with his hand cuffed to his ankle. He was loping toward the house, eager to find out what had been done with the intruder.

Maybe this milkman would be the one to carry on Stan Milque's grand plan, Remo thought.

Not if he had anything to say about it. And he did.

Remo stepped out of the truck and found another projectile. Not a grain of sand this time—it was a rock, as big as a golf ball. He felt its shape, he weighed it in his hand to get the measure of its density and mass distribution, then he tossed it.

The surviving mercenary heard the whistle of scorched wind and thought he saw the man who had attacked him earlier—and a streak of gray matter heading in his direction, and then the rock tore into his chest and exploded out of his back.

Remo felt no better. He just wanted to leave this ugliness behind him.

He drove away.

3

Lance Belmont was in desperate need of a drink. He'd been looking for booze for hours, and he just couldn't believe there was none to be found.

"Look," he said insistently to the native boy with the dirty hair and the tray of bootleg suntan lotions. "U.S. dollars. See? That's a U.S. president. That's the one that got shot. You know it must be a valuable bill if we put our most famous dead president on it. Worth a lot."

"Worth five bucks," the young Haitian man answered. "Five bucks can't be that much to a man like you."

"Look, all I'm asking for is a drink. A cocktail. I cannot believe they don't serve cocktails anywhere in the village."

"Believe it. They don't sell sunblock, either. Got some Copper-Skin SPF 99 for you. That you can buy for twenty bucks."

"What kind of tropical getaway is this when they don't even have tropical drinks?"

"It is not meant to be a getaway. It is meant to be kind of a *hounfo,* kind of like. You know, a congregation. A place of worship, man."

Lance Belmont tried to keep his cool. "I understand that. Don't get me wrong. I love this place. And I love the Priestess. But when I came here, I didn't know that it was dry."

The Haitian smiled. It was not a friendly smile, and yet Lance felt reassured when the young man put a hand on his shoulder and nodded as if in understanding. "Don't you worry. You look around long enough, you'll find some hooch."

Lance's pulse quickened. "Really?"

"Maybe. Eventually. But what you really need is some sunblock."

"I don't want any fucking sunblock!"

Lance Belmont had not counted on this. You come here, to the tropics, even if it is goddamn Haiti, and you expect to be able to buy what you want. He had lots of frickin' money. The people who lived around here had nothing. He could not understand why it was so difficult to buy himself a little bootleg rum.

Lance had his faith in humanity and the world restored in short order. The young Haitian man was one of the hangers around the village, and not one of the locals who were part of the village itself.

The merchants were the Haitians who could not bring themselves to worship the Priestess's way. That did not mean that they were averse to helping supply the village with its needs.

The small village deep in the old-growth mangrove preserve had become a destination for wealthy Americans. Even without a beach or tennis court, the private plot of land had the people flocking in—and staying. You came here to live, not to vacation.

It was a religious sanctuary. The Priestess owned the land and ran the religious services, which were part voodoo and part something else. Nobody really understood it, but that didn't stop the Americans from streaming in. The free-love aspect had something to do with the appeal.

Even some Haitians had moved into the village and joined the flock. Those who were not a part of the flock were not allowed to enter the village grounds. They kept at the fringes, kept a low profile among the mangrove swamps and let the villagers come to them.

Lance was wandering the long circle of the village just to pass the time. The pleasure pavilions couldn't entice him. The aromas from the five-times-a-day buffet made him feel ill. How could he think about food when he needed alcohol?

Then one of the old-timers stumbled into him. The man was a recently retired used-car salesman, and he had the benefit of a whole week in the village. He was still wearing a polyester golf shirt and shiny acrylic pants, which were rank in the ninety-five-degree heat and ninety-five percent humidity. But he had another smell that was even more pungent—a booze smell.

"Sorry, buddy," mumbled the car salesman. His eyes rolled into his head. He was thoroughly intoxicated.

"Where'd you get the booze?" Belmont demanded.

"Said I was sorry." The car salesmen couldn't even figure out what Belmont was talking about. Belmont explained slowly that he wanted to buy some alcohol.

"Try the booze sellers," the car salesman suggested.

Belmont was on the verge of French kissing the old son of a bitch just to inhale some of the high-proof fumes coming out of his gullet. "Where are the booze sellers?"

"I'll show you."

The salesman wandered back the way he had come, stumbling frequently. Most of the village was paved with old stone set in the earth, or there were new wooden walkways over the rough terrain. Elsewhere, the earth was dangerous with exposed mangrove roots.

They came to an open area with many buildings and lots of walking trails leading in all directions. The drunk was having trouble remembering the way. Belmont was not surprised. He still had no idea how to find his way around the maze of clearings and passages and patches of marshland that made up the topography of the village. But he also had zero patience at this point. He needed a drink and he needed it now.

"I thought it was this way," the drunk muttered.

"Well, it's not," Belmont snapped. "So which way is it?"

The drunk pointed to a big mangrove tree, then another, put his fist to his mouth to hold down whatever was threatening to come up, and swallowed it. He said, "I could have sworn it was this way."

Then the drunk seemed to have a revelation. "I remember now. Look for the palace of the Priestess. Then go as far away from there as you can. That's where you leave the village and find the booze guy."

Belmont had been here for half a day and had seen nothing to qualify as a palace. All he had seen were hundred-year-old stone buildings and recently erected, primitive-looking studio condos. Lance now owned one of these condos, but he hadn't bothered to check it out yet.

First things first.

"Okay, so where's the palace?"

"I don't know," the drunk said. "But it's easy to spot."

The drunk tried to tightrope walk up the twisting roots of a mangrove, and made windmills when his balance was about to fail, but then he grabbed the trunk of the tree and managed to stabilize himself long enough to scan the village in all directions.

He gestured to Belmont. "Up here. You can see it."

Belmont climbed up the tangled roots, wondering how the drunk had done it. It was precarious enough for an unpleasantly sober man such as himself. The roots took him five feet off the ground and he peered through the trees, and spotted a building of bleached stone looming up out of the old mangroves, maybe a mile away through the village.

"The palace of the Priestess," the drunk said. "They say she never leaves it."

"Except for the ceremonies," Belmont added, not caring.

"Yeah," the drunk said, nodding solemnly, trying to keep the booze from backing up on him and failing. "She does come out for the ceremonies. That's what I hear, anyway. But I also hear that she doesn't take part in the demonstrations of devotion, if you know what I mean."

Belmont did not know what he meant and he didn't care.

"They also say that she's the one you'd most want to get down and devoted with. If you know what I mean."

Belmont was more concerned with satisfying his own devotions at the moment. The drunk, with some urging, stumbled down the roots and took Belmont through the village, the routes taking them in the opposite direction from the palace of the Priestess. They passed a hundred small, primitive-looking huts. They were mostly four-unit condos made with unfinished wooden floors, stucco walls and thatched roofs.

At the far end of the village was another clearing, but this was the trashy end of the settlement. No condos here. Still, there were a lot of people stumbling around sipping sunblock out of the bottle.

"Go to the far end. Farthest that you can go. That's where they are, 'bout twenty yards into the swamp. Just give 'em your bottle and they'll fill it up for you. Don't say anything."

"I don't have a bottle."

The drunk squinted at him. "Well, how d'you expect to carry around some booze?"

"Booze usually comes in its own container."

"Back in the States, maybe. Not here."

"How am I supposed to know that?"

"Live and learn. This is bootleg hooch. They ain't got no bottles. And you can't walk around the village with your liquor out in the open anyway." The drunk cast his eyes at the ground. "The Leatherhead man will take it away."

"Can I have your bottle? You've had enough for one morning, anyway."

The drunk said, "Hokay. Fifty bucks."

"Fifty! The kid back there was selling them for twenty."

"Then buy from him."

Lance wasn't going to waste the precious minutes it would take to return to the central clearing and then get back to the ass end of the village. "Fine. Here." He thrust a bunch of fives at the drunk, but when the drunk took them, Belmont grasped the bottom half of the stack and slipped it away before the drunk noticed.

The drunk shoved the bills in his pants and grabbed his sunblock bottle out of his hip pocket. There was a trickle of booze still sloshing around inside. He upended it and squirted it into his mouth.

It was just a little more than he could handle. He thrust the bottle at Belmont then staggered to a mangrove tree to upchuck behind the roots.

Pretty disgusting, Lance thought, then scooted quickly into the swamp to get his sunblock bottle filled.

4

"She summons the dawn and she is the lover of life."

"But what it is the purpose of this worship?" the reporter asked.

"It is to celebrate life," the starry-eyed young woman said breathlessly. "We celebrate the Priestess's love of life. She's summons the dawn of life."

"There are rumors of all kinds of strange activity at the village of the Priestess," the reporter said.

"By *strange* you mean, our expressions of love? You mean, our nonstop festival of joy? We love and we dance and taste the fruits of the earth. This you call strange?"

"Oh, not me," the reporter said sincerely. "I'm a reporter for Alpha Network News. My journalistic integrity prevents me from having any kind of emotional involvement that might lead me to have any kind of opinion about your activities. Our news coverage is always one-hundred-percent impartial. Can you be more descriptive about the nature of the various forms of sin and immoral behavior that goes into your aberrant revelry?"

The young woman folded her hands on her lap. She was in her late teens or early twenties, with the milk-white skin and gleaming brown hair of a Midwestern farmer's daughter. And she had the endearing habit of tucking a loose stray of those gleaming brown locks behind one ear. They were at the table of a Fort Lauderdale ocean-side hotel. "I don't even know what sin is," she said.

"I believe there is more to it than you're letting on," the reporter said. He fished into his briefcase and plopped an eight-by-ten on the table. He tapped the middle of the image sharply with one finger and said, "Perhaps you can tell me what I should make of this?"

The young woman pushed the lock of hair behind her ear. "I can't make out anything," she said.

"Oh, really? It was taken in the village."

"But it is all black," the girl said.

"Not all black," the reporter said. He indicated the top right quadrant of the photo. "If you look closely, you can clearly see what I'm talking about."

"I'm sorry," she said. "Why don't you tell me what *you* think is in the picture."

"Mass fornication, young lady. This proves it."

"It does?"

"We have a reporter on the grounds of the Priestess's village. Our reporter reported that this sort of public behavior is common in the village. We're having this photo digitally enhanced. We'll splash it all over the world. You might as well come clean."

"You want me to tell you there is widespread love among those who dwell with the Priestess?" The young woman was amused. "All right. I am telling you that."

The reporter's eyes shifted. "Are you saying the rumors about the orgies are true?"

"They're not rumors. They're in our press release. They went out to all the networks an hour ago."

"What?" The reporter's tongue felt dry.

"We sent photos, too." The glint in her eyes had become mischievous. "Much better than yours. See?"

She produced a tube of pages from her back pocket, unrolling them to reveal a crisp, vivid image of a tiny town in the mangrove preserve. The grass was sprinkled with diamond-like dew alongside stone walkways, neat wooden bridgeways and neat, clean-looking huts. There were happy people chatting on the wooden bridges, but they weren't as happy as those gathered in a screened pavilion in the background. The reporter couldn't count them all, but he could see what they were doing, even with the screen giving the activities a gray blur.

What horrified the reporter most was the legend at the bottom of the photo.

"Copyrighted for exclusive use by:" said the stamp, and underneath was the penned-in name of a rival news network.

The second shot was from another angle, offering a clearer view of the interior of the pavilion. There were people. Intertwined, naked, sweaty people. Digital blurs disguised the ecstatic faces and other objectionable body parts. Exclusively for another network entirely.

All the shots were vivid, and not one of them was designated for Alpha Network News.

"We did not have a contact at Alpha," the young woman explained reasonably.

"I've been calling you people for weeks!" the reporter squeaked.

"But you were impolite," the girl said. "You are all so inflexible and you have such a skewed agenda."

"Skewed agenda? Who's the slut here, anyway?" The reporter clamped his hand over his mouth. "Sorry. Sorry. I'll try to be more polite. So can I have a picture?" he asked desperately.

"You already have pictures."

Both of them glanced down at the black, muddy print that might or might not show an act of fornication somewhere, compared to the brilliant, crisp shot of the orgy in the pavilion.

The reporter's heart sank. Those pictures had been at the heart of his exposé on the Cult of the Dawn. He had been working it for months, and Alpha Network News had been hyping the exposé with one-minute spots all week. He had called the cult's U.S. representatives over and over, seeking an interview with the head of the cult, the woman known only as the Priestess of the Dawn. The cult reps asked him in the mildest terms not to publish his photos. The reporter knew he had them on the ropes then.

"They're going on the news whether you like it or not. You want to at least explain yourself, I'm giving you the chance."

For the first time, the cult agreed to an interview with the Alpha Network News reporter. It was in the evening, not twenty-four hours before the scheduled broadcast of his exposé.

But the cult had played him for a fool. They gave all the other networks the good photos. Everybody but him. And their timing was perfect.

"Oh, Christ!" He jumped to the hotel room television and flipped it on, scanning the channels. They all had the cult pictures—every network except Alpha Network News. Alpha had nothing.

There was no way he could go on the air with his black, muddy shots that may or may not be people doing it, somewhere. His exposé was canceled. Alpha would be the laughingstock of the news media—again. The reporter would bear the brunt of the blame and almost certainly lose his job.

"I'm done for," he decided miserably. "You ruined me."

She gave him an "oh, really?" smile.

"Can't you give me something?" he begged. "Anything?"

"How about a gift certificate for a free condo?"

The reporter was stunned. "A free *condominium?* You mean, in the village? You're giving it to me?"

"The Priestess has lots of them standing empty. Retail value is one hundred, twenty-five thousand dollars. Want it?" She dangled a gift certificate printed on heavy paper stock.

"You're trying to tempt me into a life of sin and fornication."

"Call it what you like. I call it paradise."

The reporter looked conflicted. "I guess my wife'll kick me out anyway if my career goes down the crapper."

"I'd love to see you there," the young spokeswoman said.

The reporter's eyes became shifty. "If I took you up on it, would we be able to meet up? You know—hang out together?"

"Hang out? Sure. But I was hoping we could get naked together in the pleasure pavilion."

The report nodded like a nervous chimp. "Oh. Sure, that would be okay, too."

5

CURE was not an acronym; it was the actual name of a small agency of the United States' federal government that operated for years out of the same office in the private hospital in New York. Smith had been its director from the start.

After a distinguished career in U.S. intelligence, Smith was about to retire from the CIA when he got a call from the President of the United States. The President in those days was young, idealistic and beloved, but he had come to an unpleasant realization. The United States' constitutional democracy was not working.

It was not working because the rights and freedoms spelled out in the Constitution were used against the nation. Small-time crooks gridlocked the courts, claiming their rights were being violated. Killers were freed on legal technicalities. The more time a felon served, the better he became at manipulating the legal system and escaping punishment for even the most heinous of crimes.

The young President—who was a man fated to be assassinated, his shooting watched again and again around the world—had a bold plan. Harold W. Smith did not like the plan.

The plan called for forming an organization that would protect the people of the U.S.A. by ignoring their constitutional rights. Violate their privacy to convict the criminals. If this activity could be carried out in total secrecy, under the control of a man with unquestioned loyalty to this country, then it could do tremendous good.

Smith agreed to take on the role of director of the new organization. He was a patriot and as such he could never refuse a request from the President of the United States.

There was another reason he took the job: his conviction that he could take on such a huge responsibility and not abuse the power that came with it, but anyone else the President might choose for the job would not succumb to the lure of power. Smith understood a little about human nature, and he understood himself and, with all humbleness, he knew he was quite simply one of the most trustworthy people in the U.S. government.

CURE succeeded in funneling intelligence to

law-enforcement offices across the country, but it was unable to stem the tide of lawlessness by pushing papers.

Smith had become a believer in CURE, and in what it did for America, but he thought long and hard before taking the next step in CURE's evolution. Finally, he came to believe that CURE needed an enforcement arm, someone who could get in and take care of the problems that the police or the FBI could not. Someone who was loyal to the United States and who possessed the skills required to carry out assassinations.

That was where Remo Williams came in. Smith applied the code name "Destroyer." Smith never had—and never would—understand how fully the name applied to Remo.

SINCE ITS INCEPTION, CURE had been headquartered in Folcroft Sanitarium in Rye, New York. Harold W. Smith served as the director of Folcroft, as well as director of CURE.

The doors to his Folcroft office came open at approximately 11:35 p.m.

"Check this out, Smitty," Remo said, slapping the newspaper on the glass desktop.

"Good evening, Wise Emperor, "Chiun said. It was Chiun's custom to refer to the CURE director as Emperor. His reason was based on tradition. The Masters of Sinanju allowed their services to be contracted only to state leaders with true power. Kings and emperors had all paid for the assassination skills of the Masters. The emperors of China had employed the Masters, as had pharaohs, khans and tsars. When the silly and transient democracies began to pop into existence, the Masters made allowances and allowed themselves to be hired by the so-called presidents and the alleged prime ministers. However, to allow oneself to be employed by a mere director was unacceptable. Chiun's rationale was that Smith did, in fact, possess the power of an emperor. He simply chose—foolishly, in Chiun's mind—not to exercise that power. Chiun therefore referred to Smith as emperor and his heir apparent, Mark Howard, assistant director of CURE, as Prince.

Smith had resisted the title vigorously for years, but finally gave up and accepted it.

"Look," Remo insisted, stabbing the newspaper with his finger. Kimonos Are Kuul On The Coast said the headline. "I couldn't help but notice the rise in this new fashion among the kids these days."

"I have been monitoring the situation," Smith said. "I am surprised you follow the fashion world, Remo. What do you make of it?"

"I would say it is an interesting trend," Remo said. "Wait, *trend* is not the word I'm looking for. It's more like a movement."

"I see," Smith said. "You think it's important?"

"Sure. Really important."

"And you, Master Chiun?" Smith asked. "What are your thoughts on the situation?"

"Obviously, the Western world will latch on to any cultural aberration, regardless of its provenance and without regard to its meaning. In this case, like all others, they have done so. It is meaningless to the fashion junkers. And yet beneficial."

Smith narrowed his vision. "Beneficial?"

"Fortuitous."

Smith considered that. "Fortuitous?"

"Providential," Chiun suggested.

Remo was wondering when he had lost track of this conversation. But he was certain he had lost track.

"Hey, where's Junior?" At times like this, it always seemed to him that the assistant director of CURE could help him bridge the communication gap.

"On sick leave," Smith said offhandedly, and disingenuously.

"Sick leave? You've never given anybody sick leave before."

Chiun glared at Remo to silence him and announced, "What my son has done, he did for me. His heart, at least, is in the right place."

"Master Chiun, what exactly did Remo do?"

"Caused this to happen," Chiun explained, sweeping a hand grandly at the paper.

Smith gaped at them. "But why?"

"What do you mean, why?" Remo asked. "You are the one who gave Chiun the idea. You're the one giving him so much flak about the robes and stuff."

"The robes?"

"The kimonos," Remo said, exasperated.

"What does this have to do with kimonos?"

"When exactly is Junior gonna be back from sick leave?" Remo said.

"It may be many days."

"Maybe we should come back then and finish talking about it."

"Why don't you explain to me what it is you are talking about," Smith said.

"You know, Chiun's business venture. He's become a kimono importer. You gotta know about this, Smitty. He's been at it for months."

"I know of it," Smith said. "I have been following his business centers with some interest. But, I must say, Master Chiun, that you have found some unique ways of bypassing international shipping registration procedures and fees. You clearly have a head for business."

Chiun smiled and nodded slightly.

"The venture will be worthwhile if it achieves its purpose," Chiun said. "My purpose was not to make a profit."

"Which makes the venture even more intriguing," Smith said. "Still, what has this to do with the article in the newspaper?"

"Read it," Remo said. "Kimonos are what the article in the newspaper is about."

Smith looked from one to the other, then turned back to the newspaper.

Smith said, "I see. But this is not the matter that concerns me. I speak of a different issue raised by the newspaper."

Smith unceremoniously folded over the pages, burying the kimonos article. "What concerns me is *this*."

Remo glanced at the article, about some new sort of cult in Haiti. He was interested not at all. He took the paper and folded it back to the original page and showed the kimonos article.

"This is what we're talking about."

"I understand that you are pleased with the success of the venture," Smith said patiently. "And yet, it is of little consequence in the overall scheme of things." Smith folded it back to the article about a new wave of Haitian religious zealots. "This is higher on my priority list."

Chiun pursed his lips. Remo snatched the newspaper from Smith's fingers and used his short but sharp fingernails. The small office of CURE filled with a cloud of paper particles that billowed in all directions before drifting gently to the floor. Smith started to say something, but the miniscule pieces of newsprint entered his lungs. He coughed and flung one arm across his face, breathing through the fabric of his suit jacket sleeve.

When the confetti cleared the air, his eyes were bright red and watery. The office was covered with a powder coating of confetti, like the beautiful dusting of snow on a winter's morning.

The original newspaper had completely disappeared except for a carefully trimmed article resting on Smith's desk. It was the article about the kimono trend in Trenton.

"Where is Chiun?" Smith coughed.

"Where do you think he this? Just think about this for a moment, Smitty. Remember your 'kimonos being of little consequence' remark? I can't think of the last time you were such a jerk."

"Surely, Master Chiun knows I wasn't being deliberately insulting. What I said was the truth—there are issues at this moment more important than his fashion enterprise."

"Yeah, well, what is truth, anyway? What is true to you isn't necessarily true to everybody else. Sure not to Chiun."

"But this is an important matter," Smith insisted, trying to remain perfectly still, since every small movement stirred up the newsprint dust.

"That doesn't really matter, does it? What matters to Chiun is that you've told him that the most important thing he's done in months is of little consequence."

"But Chiun downplayed it himself," Smith objected. "He was just telling me there was no profit in it!"

"Right. No profit, but he went and did it anyway. Why do you suppose he did that anyway? Think he wants to market Asian culture to the world?"

Smith sighed. "I do understand, Remo. I know this has something to do with his desire to continue wearing his kimonos in the field. I am sure he has successfully engineered a kimono fashion and now it's acceptable for him to continue wearing them. I suppose I never seriously believed that I could convince him to stop wearing them anyway. Does that settle the matter?"

"Sure, for me it does. But you know, Smitty, what

little people skills you used to have, you're losing the older you get."

"Perhaps," Smith said, and slid the remaining newspaper clipping across his desk to the far corner, then moved his foot to activate the computer display mounted beneath the glass desktop. "Let us move on to the issue at hand."

The news clipping had moved back into the center of the desk, blocking most of the computer display. Smith had not even seen Remo put it there. "*We* came to see *you*, remember. You did not call us. This is *our* meeting. This is what the meeting is about."

"But with Master Chiun not present, we may not conclude the issue," Smith said.

"Cripes, you're such a sour-ass," Remo said. "How can you keep getting me so peeved after all this time? You must really try hard. But that's nothing compared to Chiun. I have the feeling he's really ticked off. Thanks for agreeing to see us. You're a great boss."

To Smith's alarm, the newspaper clipping had vanished from his desk and Remo had vanished from his office. The door was wide open and beginning to close, stirring up the fine dust of newspaper shred—Remo's departure had stirred none.

"Remo, please come back."

The door closed. Smith heaved a long sigh into the dust.

"Hey, I'm the one who gets to be exasperated here," Remo said. Smith spun in his seat to find the Reigning Master of Sinanju standing at the window that looked out over Long Island Sound. "Okay, I am back. What you want?"

"I wish to speak now about this other matter," Smith said. Then added, "May we move on to this other matter?"

"Go ahead. Your careless insults are forgotten. I said that, didn't I?"

Smith squeezed his eyes momentarily. If Remo was right about one thing, it was that Smith was getting older and his patience was getting shorter. For how many years had he been trying to make sense of the erratic personalities of his enforcement arm. It was a constant challenge simply to get Remo to listen, or to keep Chiun from taking offense. Every meeting with the pair of strained his tolerance more and more. What was most frustrating was that Smith could not tell if it was truly himself becoming less reasonable or Remo and Chiun growing increasingly obstinate.

Quite possibly it was both.

Smith brought up a newspaper article about the Haitian cult on his screen—essentially the same article that was now drifting about his office in tiny slivers. Remo leaned over to read it.

"What do you think?" Smith said.

"I hate Haiti."

"Have you read the complete article, Remo? It is a new religious venture that came into being on a private estate in a protected mangrove preserve on the south coast of Haiti. It appears to be founded on voodoo, and it has some voodoo ceremonial traditions. The cult is attracting worshipers from the United States, Europe, even Canada."

"Not Canada!"

Smith ignored the comment. "It is clearly a privately funded, profit-making venture. The organizers of the church require surrender of investments and financial commitments by the practitioners. Those who joined the church have an initiation fee based on their income assets."

"Don't they all?"

"There is no need to be crass, Remo."

"What's the problem? Are they killing people?"

"In fact, it looks as if they are. There's an indication that some worshipers are disappearing after their assets have been surrendered to the church. That is not what concerns me."

"What is it that concerns you?"

"The name of the cult concerns me. It is called Remo."

"Remo? Remo the Cult? The Cult of Remo? What's it stand for?"

"As far as we can tell, it stands for nothing. It is, as you said, simply the Church of Remo.

"We do not know. I do not know. I have investigated as much as possible in the past few hours. I have come up with nothing. The Church of Remo is a complete mystery. Their activities are strange, to say the least. I cannot ascertain what they are trying to accomplish, if anything more than profit."

"What is any church trying to accomplish? But why call it Remo?" Remo asked. "The Church of Remo doesn't exactly roll off the tongue."

"I agree. This is what we need to find out."

"Crap," Remo said. "I hate Haiti. And I'm sick of the Caribbean. You know, if you'd told me at our first meeting after my electrocution that I'd have to spend half my damn career in the Caribbean, I may have just decided to be dead again. Union Island ingrates. Blow-hards in the Bahamas. If it's not the pirates of the Caribbean, it's the Dutchman in freakin' St. Martin. Why don't I ever get to go to the North Pole any more? I own a real nice windbreaker."

Smith allowed the diatribe to pass, knowing that if he interrupted the flow of complaints he'd regret it and there would be only more lost time as they belabored the point.

"Yes, Remo, I need you to go to Haiti to figure out the basis for the name of this Church of Remo. It seems highly unlikely that it has anything to do with you, and yet, Remo is not that common a name."

"But there are other Remos out there," Remo protested. "There was that guy on the reality show. He was more famous than me. It's probably a church to him. Why not send him to Haiti to check it out?"

Smith said, "I believe that Remo is deceased, and I seriously doubt the cult was named after the figure of minor importance from a reality show that survives only in syndication. The name probably has nothing to do with you, either, Remo. But it may be."

"Why would it be?" Remo asked.

"To send us a message."

"Such as what?"

"I don't know. Maybe it is a way for an enemy to draw you in."

"A trap?" Remo said. "You're right. I can't risk it. I better stay home."

"We cannot afford to ignore it if it is a signal," Smith said. "It will be little effort for you to go to the cult's base and assess the situation."

"Then can I kill everybody? It's my job, you know. Assassin. It says so on my business card. My business card, by the way, is a scroll in Korean. I'll translate it for you if you really want. Why not send Junior? Or send Sarah. She doesn't really have anything to do around here anyway, right? Make her useful."

"Ms. Slate is away recovering from an illness."

Remo slit his eyes at Smith. Remo could take the measure of a man's respiration and calculate his pulse at a glance and count the microscopic drops of perspiration oozing from a man's pores.

Most of the time, Remo knew when a man was telling the truth or telling a lie. Smith was not most men and his perpetually sour disposition made him difficult to read, even to a Master of Sinanju.

Still, Remo could tell he was being fed a line of partial truths. What was up with Sarah? And Junior, for that matter?

"I predict that you will find no significance to the name of the cult, and that you will be on the ground for just a matter of hours. But we cannot ignore this situation." He gave Remo information on his flights from New York to Miami, Miami to the Dominican Republic, which was where members of the Church of Remo typically landed on the Island of Hispaniola for an overland bus trip into Haiti and to the south coast's old-growth-mangrove preserve. Smith had two seats reserved on the flights.

"I doubt Chiun's going to be embarking on secret-agent missions with me for a while, Smitty. I'm guessing he's mad as hell at you. I'll leave him here for you to deal with, okay?"

And then Remo vanished again. The door was open and as it swung closed it gave new life to the newsprint confetti, which billowed like movie fog around the office.

Smith waited for the door to latch shut, then turned in a complete circle in his chair, even glancing under his desk and rising in his seat to look for anything unusual under the desk belonging to Mark Howard, his assistant. Smith convinced himself he was completely alone.

Harold Smith sat back down, breathing through his sleeve again for minutes. He was trapped in his seat until the early morning hours when the janitorial staff of Folcroft Sanitarium could be summoned with a vacuum cleaner.

6

Joey Wild was once voted Most Likely to Go Wild.
That had been in his senior year at high school. He
followed his destiny at college, adopting the lifestyle
of the consummate fraternity party animal. There
was alcoholic bingeing and there were all-night par-
ties with crazy women and lots of uppers. He did an
admirable job of meeting the expectations of his
former classmates, especially since he didn't belong to a fraternity and was in fact attending the two-
year rural community college where most of the
students majored in agricultural science.

All he had to show for his four years at the two-
year college was an associate degree in agricultural
management. He fell into an assistant bookkeeper
position at a feedlot. That it was one of the biggest
feedlots in northwestern Georgia impressed no
one.

Ten years later he was the head accountant for the

same feedlot, keeping the books, cooking them here and there. His minor embezzlement stemmed less from a need for money and more from the need for something stimulating. He was bored. Bored with his job, his life, his wife, his house, his car.

His wife was bored, too, and found a more interesting accountant to live with. Someone who had an honest-to-god bachelor's degree. His wife and the big shot with the B.A. kicked Joey Wild out of his own house, and he found himself in a rented apartment.

The apartment was home to lots of attractive women his own age, but they were of no interest to him. He had no use for another version of his soon-to-be-former wife.

His best friend was the television. He would come home each evening and park himself in front of it, a beer in one hand, a remote control in the other, and he would start surfing.

He would click through channel after channel, hour after hour, and if he was lucky he would find something interesting enough to hold his attention for fifteen minutes at a time. Hours later he would go to bed feeling miserable and unfulfilled.

But he couldn't seem to break the habit. The guy once voted Most Likely to Go Wild was nothing but a couch potato.

It all changed one evening, right around 8:37 p.m., when his accounting skills kicked in unexpectedly and unpleasantly.

Joey Wild considered that he had 267 channels on his digital cable network, and he wondered how many times he went through the entire lineup on an average evening, typically starting at six-thirty and ending at ten-thirty.

Wild settled on twenty-eight complete rotations. That was depressing. But his mind kept working on the problem.

He calculated 7,476 channel changes on an average night. That was…what? Less than two seconds per channel change, on average. When he got going, he could flip through channels a hell of a lot faster than that. A quarter-second a channel change. He could actually go as fast as the digital cable box could keep up with him.

Fridays and Saturdays still qualified as party nights in some part of his mind, and he stayed up until twelve-thirty, maybe even one-thirty. Saturday and Sunday afternoons were almost always spent in front of the TV, either at home or at Mike's Beer Place. But Joey went to the Beer Place less often now. It was a waste of time sitting there watching shows somebody else picked.

They were losers at Mike's, but on that fateful

Wednesday evening it became clear as crystal who the biggest loser was. Joe Wild. The guy who went through, on average, 82,137 channel changes a week.

His mind reeled in blackness, but the numbers inexorably continued to plug themselves into the spreadsheet in his mind, even as his finger convulsively snapped the channel up button on the remote control.

"60 Skankiest Country Stars of the Seventies."

"Child Stars at War: Bradies on the Battlefield."

"Mayberry RFD."

"Chef Warfare Battle: Wood Pulp."

"Lose. Weight. Or Die!"

There was a part of his mind that was so perfectly trained to process the information on the screen that he could instantly assess the television program. Most of them he had glimpsed thousands of times before, and always judged them to be without interest.

"Monster Woodworking."

"Fright Factor: Kids Terrifying Kids."

"ABC News."

He tried to concentrate on the news, but his finger pulsed and the channel changed. There was a commercial for a diet plan with hideous women congregating around a storefront display of Italian pastries and licking their lips. On the next channel was a close-up of the deep valley of a female rap star's cleavage.

Just as his finger continued to snap through channels, his mind was working and he couldn't make it stop. It was seventy-four weeks since his divorce, and that came to a whopping 6,078,138 channel changes.

And in all that time, he couldn't remember ever truly watching a television show that he really enjoyed. He really didn't like TV.

So why the hell did he plant himself in front of the television night after night, weekend after weekend? What could compel a person to churn through six million channels if he knew there would be nothing on?

"Catch It and Eat It: Chigger Challenge."

"Deflowered, Season Four: Where No Man Has Gone Before."

"Professional Football."

"Disgusting Abodes."

It had to stop. He had to get out of this rut right now.

Joey reeled from the need to escape the television trap and astonishment at his own obsession. It established a strange dichotomy in his mind. At once he developed an iron resolve not only to break away, but also the determination that he would find the key to his future on the television. He would find it now. He would have to pull *something* of value out of seventy-four weeks of waste.

Joey Wild, for the first time in seventy-four weeks, began truly watching the channels as he flipped through them. This time, he watched with a purpose. His entire future, he was confident, would soon appear on his screen.

His finger removed itself from the button when he landed on a cable shopping network. There was a magnificent woman, a pageant star from decades past, who had fought back the ravages of time with surgery and injections. Her hair was an unnatural banana-yellow and her eyes were pulled away from the middle of her face by tension from the surgical removal of extra flesh on the sides of her face. Her lips were swollen, as if she had been in a bar fight just before coming on the air, and were shellacked with some kind of cosmetic slime.

On the table before her were CD cases and printed brochures, and the hideous woman described a lifestyle of flamboyance and wealth that was sure to come to all who purchased the program.

The program she offered was apparently a new twist on held real-estate schemes.

"Billions of dollars from the federal government

are being doled out to rich, undeserving companies, some of them not even from this country. By taking your own slice of the federal cash cow, you are not only helping Americans, you are helping to secure our country, and getting rich, too!"

Next came the image of a man in a cherry-red Jaguar, driving through the ruins of a south Alabama neighborhood. The next shot showed a young, slick-looking man sitting on the front end of the Jaguar and pushing his sunglasses higher onto his nose. "I got a loan from the feds to buy my own construction company. Now I am getting all kinds of federal contracts to rebuild two whole blocks of this town. I'm living the life I always knew I deserved and helping these poor folks get their own lives back in order."

Joey Wild tapped the plastic side of the remote control, considering this option. Was this what the television had intended for him to see? Sure, he would work a cheesy construction scheme. But what was the value in it? How would it change his life?

He decided this was not the answer. He didn't need a career. He had a career. What he needed was a purpose.

With new clarity to his life's priorities, he touched the remote control button again. There were more reality shows. None seemed to have much promise for him. He landed on a reality program about private fraud investigators. Wild was amused to note that they were investigating programs promising to get buyers rich on federal contracts.

Maybe this was what he was looking for. Maybe he could find a life for himself in exposing the weaknesses of others. He could use his accounting skills to expose fraud and embezzlement across corporate America. He knew how to find fraud. He had uncovered fraud and committed fraud within his own company. He would be the belligerent corporate auditor. He would confront overpaid executives on tape with evidence of their improprieties.

At the end of every program he would tell his viewers to alert him to fraud within their own companies. Every company had employees with inside knowledge of impropriety. His successes would breed bigger successes. Soon, he would graduate to Enron-size financial debacles. He would be feared across the corporate world. What satisfaction there would be in cowing the reigning princes of America.

But then Joey Wild found that his finger had poked the channel up button, as if with a mind of its own.

Next came a weight-loss infomercial, founded on a system of exercises using a variety of equipment. Apparently, the marketers had taken possession of the leftover product lines of several other failed exercise infomercial marketing schemes and come up with an ingenious plan to dispose of them.

Their weight-loss plan required an investment of just ninety-nine dollars, and the company would ship the customer a new piece of exercise equipment each and every week. By following the scientifically designed exercise itinerary and following the easy meal plan, the customer was guaranteed to transform from obese to beautiful in five weeks. Keeping it off was even easier—the company would continue to ship new exercise equipment once a month for a low annual fee.

Getting in shape was one of Joey Wild's most important lifetime goals, but he didn't think that this infomercial was the future he was looking for.

He clicked again. He had gone through most of the channels already, and soon he was going to have to find his answer.

He wouldn't allow himself to do the dreaded channel loop again, not ever. He would find the answer to his life on one of the remaining channels and then he would drop the remote control in the garbage disposal.

All he was seeing was cooking shows and home modeling shows, and breathless documentaries that promised to expose the truth about the pope, the Holy Grail, moon landings and the theory of relativity. There was nothing there for him.

And he was only twenty channels from the end of the lineup.

He slowed his channel changing, giving full value to each and every channel regardless of its content. There was an old, old nun mumbling the rosary. Wild thought she could use a good weight-loss and diet program. Next came a gardening show, explaining how normally ungainly varieties of shrubs could be trained, through the use of wires, ropes and strategic overapplication of nitrogen fertilizer, to remain in an aesthetically pleasing stunted state.

Joey Wild was desperate. Three channels left. With a trembling finger he hit the button once. For the love of God, it was a test pattern. It was the access station for his old alma mater, the local community college.

Normally, it might have been showing class schedules or advertising new student programs. Maybe there could have been some sort of a new academic field that would have served as Joe Wild's path to the future, but it was nothing but the test pattern. Still he studied it. It was only the name of the community college. Was it telling him that he should go back to community college? Should he teach accounting at the local community college? Maybe that was it. He would teach community college accounting to little hick babes without enough cash or smarts to get into a four-year college, and spend the rest of his life trading grades for favors. It was his best option so far.

But it wasn't a great option. There was just one channel left.

He was afraid to press the channel up button again. He felt he was committing himself to whatever was on the very last channel. Channel 514 was the last channel, and Wild tried to remember what programs were on Channel 514.

How could he *not* know what Channel 514 was? He had seen Channel 514 more than three hundred times a week for seventy-four weeks. He had been on that channel more than 23,800 times.

He didn't believe he didn't know what was there. The human mind could not be exposed to that kind of repetition without the knowledge burning itself in.

Joey Wild knew what was on Channel 514, but he couldn't make the knowledge reveal itself.

He closed his eyes and visualized. Click. Click. Click. He pictured the baggy nun. She was always on a few channels back. Click. He visualized the community college. Click. He visualized…*what?*

He visualized Cable Access Infotainment. But that was Channel 1. But he knew there was one more channel on the lineup. So Channel 514 may have been added lately. Channels came and went all the time. But it meant that Channel 514 was an unknown entity.

Could fate—the same fate that had convinced Joey Wild that his future was here on his television—have also engineered the new channel? Was Channel 514 put there just for him? To steer him on his new path?

With his luck, it would be just another bunch of religious nuts. Or another survival-in-paradise show. Or another infomercial.

To his surprise, when he pushed the button, it was all of those things combined.

"HELLO, FRIENDS, I am Clive Rung," the man said as he crossed his arms like Superman on a movie poster, hair tossed by a warm tropical breeze. "I am here to offer you the opportunity of a lifetime. No, let me correct that—I am offering you a whole new life! Like nothing you have seen before on television, and yet, like everything you ever dreamed about on television."

Joey Wild's attention was firmly in Clive Rung's grasp. Clive Rung claimed to offer exactly what

Joey Wild was seeking. It was as if he had come on-screen and said, "Joey Wild, I will now tell you where your life is about to go."

Wild lowered the footrest of his recliner. He never watched television in this way—but he did now. He put the remote control down on the snack table, and he knew that this was it. He had found when he was looking for, in the last place he had looked.

"This is more than any vacation. This is more than any visit to church. This is more than any visit to Vegas. This is all those things rolled together. Maybe you have heard about the new wave of worship that has taken hold in the roots of the souls of so many people like you. They come from America and from around the world, and they come to taste the ecstasy that the Priestess of the Church of Remo has for them."

Joey thought he'd heard of this one. But he had heard about a lot of them. You couldn't turn around without finding one obscure cult or another advertising to bring new geese into their flock. It seemed to him that the Priestess of the Church of Remo was a little bit different. She didn't try to attract geese. She let others do it for her. She ran her little commune, out there in the islands, and let word of mouth spread.

"You've heard about the Priestess of Remo,"

Clive Rung said. "Maybe you have heard of what it is like to be a member of her worship. Well, I have been there, friends. And I can tell you it is all true. Anything you heard about, friends, well, it ain't no lie. The priestess is real. And all the rumors about how she worships is real, too. I've been there, friends. I know. I have known the bliss of being conjoined with the Priestess and her worshipers. I want to share my ecstasy with the world. And that is why I am offering you the opportunity to join the Priestess."

Then, for the benefit of those who had not heard the rumors about what occurred during the worship of the Church of Remo, Clive Rung showed them.

"First, you arrive in the tropical Caribbean. That's where I am right now, speaking to you from the beaches of Hispaniola. I want to tell you, friends, it truly is paradise."

Long shots of the wide, sandy beaches, with palm trees and turquoise water. Of tanned vacationers sunbathing on the beach chairs. Now, Joey Wild knew better than that. If he remembered correctly, the worship of the Church of Remo was nowhere near the beach. And it was not on the Dominican Republic side of the Island. The Church of Remo was in a mangrove swamp in the country of Haiti, one of the poorest nations in the hemisphere.

"The worshipers join the Priestess in her own verdant, protected settlement, and it is a village that lives by the code of the Priestess," Clive Rung enthused.

What followed were news clips that rang a bell with Joey Wild. He recalled more of what he had seen of the village of the priestess. There were lots of the blurry photos of worshipers who apparently romped naked in the village's open-air thatched pavilions. There were men walking around with two and three women clinging to them. There were the scenes of feast tables and nude dancing around bonfires.

"No one knows exactly how the Priestess attracts all these young, vibrant worshipers," Clive Rung exhorted. "But she does. She eases the souls of her worshipers and she excites their minds and bodies."

Now Joey Wild thought again of the first time he had heard about the Church of Remo. He thought it was another hedonistic vacation stand, designed to lure in horny middle-aged men. There were always clothing-optional hotels in the tropics with anything-goes sales slogans. The advertisements always showed beautiful, firm-limbed young models romping on the beach in their altogether. When you got there, you figured out pretty quick that ninety percent of the guests at the resort were not firm young models. They were saggy, middle-aged men—exactly not what you wanted to see romping around in the altogether.

The rumors, such as they were, claimed that that the Church of Remo was not like that. The church did not actively solicit guests. You did not pay to stay in the village of the Priestess. You simply went. You were simply accepted.

Joey made sure his cable box was recording the program, then ran to grab his laptop computer and began scrounging around for information regarding the Church of Remo. There were several active blog sites. There were reams of information about the church.

Not many people had been there. Everyone seemed to consider it a scam. But then, just two days ago, a news exposé had revealed the shocking truth: it was almost all true. The village was seventy percent women. Casual sex was rampant. The Priestess provided regular feasts, like a cruise ship. Every day was a party. And getting in was free.

Still, there was much reluctance to actually go there. It was in Haiti, after all. There was also the problem of lodging. The Priestess provided no accommodations. On the other hand, one could hire a local builder to put together a one-room shack in a matter of hours. Of course, this included no plumbing.

There was also a deep-seated suspicion. There had to be a catch.

The spokesperson for the Priestess, a vibrant young Kansas girl, was hit with some hard questions during her press conference a few days before. How could the Priestess support her flock when she required no payment?

Easy. Voluntary donations from worshipers were substantial and more than covered the supplies and payrolls for the big commercial kitchens. Most produce and seafood came from local Haitians at a fraction of the cost of supplies in the U.S. The land was an old Haitian estate, bought by the Priestess from a Haitian family using her personal funds. Worshipers had her permission to build small dwellings on her property. Yes, eventually the Priestess would run out of space and would halt the building of new dwellings.

The message of the press conferences was clear. If you wanted to claim your space, you better claim it soon.

On the TV, Clive Rung was explaining how he provided all the necessary arrangements for a new life at the bosom of the Priestess, starting with a chartered flight from Miami, all the documents and ground transport needed to get from the airport in the Dominican Republic to the lush nature preserve that was home to the Priestess's village. There were necessary fees to be paid to the Haitians. And in the village, Clive Rung had built a small complex of studio condominiums—and they included indoor plumbing, unlike the dwellings built by the locals. Clive Rung condos even came equipped with a small, man-powered electrical generator. "Just enough to keep your phone charged," Rung explained.

"They're not big, but they're comfy and they are yours. You don't rent them. You buy them. I give you everything you need to establish a new life in paradise. I take care of your home, your comfort, your soul, your entertainment. From there, friend, it's up to you to make the most of it. My operators are standing by."

The cost wasn't even all that bad, when you considered what you were getting. Not when you compared it to several weeks in a resort—and this was indefinite. It just so happened that Joey Wild had that much money tucked away in the bank.

He had found his answer. He wasn't sure what it was all about, but he was committed. Maybe he would find his spirituality. Maybe he'd have a few weeks of trashy sex. Maybe he would be ripped off for few thousand bucks. But he would have tried something new.

And what was the worst that could happen?

At least he would be doing something besides sitting in front of the TV.

THE SYSTEM WORKED pretty well. The chartered flight left Miami on time, and on the brief flight to the Dominican Republic the Clive Rung Travel representative explained what would happen in the next twelve hours. It was just like in the infomercial. The studio apartments were built. The Clive Rung Travel representative handed them the keys to their condos. She explained that they would be picked up and transported by chartered bus to the beautiful Haitian mangrove preserve.

They would land in Pedernales in the Dominican Republic. The bus trip was about fifty miles over a circuitous route, hugging the Hispaniola southern coast. Two hours in the bus, tops. The bus driver would personally cart their bags to their condos. No gratuities were necessary—this service was included in the package price.

"Where do we check in?" a nervous man asked. He was wearing black socks and leather sandals so new they still had the plastic tag attached to the heel.

"There is no check-in. No official notification is needed. You simply become a part of the community. You will find it is a welcoming place. What you do from then on is up to you. You do simply what you chose."

"Can we organize any events or excursions with you?" the nervous man asked.

The Clive Rung Travel representative smiled patiently.

"There are no events or excursions to organize. We are not representatives of the village or of the Priestess. We simply arrange for you to arrive safely at the village and have accommodations. What happens afterward, happens. You don't need reservations to be a part of it. All you need to do is show up."

The man in the new sandals and black socks was unsettled by this. He had not done his homework, Joey Wild decided. He didn't get it.

But it was understandable, too, since the Church of Remo didn't work the way any other place worked. You couldn't think of it like a regular hotel resort or like a regular church. Nobody recruited you; you just walked in and were there.

"But what if we find we're not welcome?" the nervous man asked.

At last. A question that did make sense. But the Clive Rung Travel representative was reassuring when she said, "Sir, all are welcome."

7

Remo found Chiun in the bedroom suite that they shared when they were at Folcroft Sanitarium. It was their home, by default, when there was no place else for them. It seemed so often during his career with CURE there had been no real home for him. For years, he slept in hotel rooms. Finally they had taken a home in an old church in Boston that was converted to condos. Remo and Chiun had shared the entire building, just the two of them, until it was destroyed by an arsonist.

And after that, there had been a duplex. Chiun had liked the place for a while. Remo never really did. He was just glad to have someplace to stay that wasn't Folcroft.

These days, Chiun seemed to regard his U.S. home as being an antique, perfectly restored Airstream camper parked at a campground in South Carolina. And the place was okay. Remo didn't mind spending time there. Chiun had rented out an entire wing, giving them lots of privacy.

The camper was okay, too, but the camper wasn't home. Neither was Folcroft. Not by a long shot. Folcroft was just familiar. Finding a new place to stay, though, would have required Chiun's approval. And that seemed like more work than it was worth, especially when Chiun seemed perfectly content with his Airstream in South Carolina.

When Remo found Chiun sitting on his reed mat, with four of his travel trunks stacked near the door of the suite, Remo knew that South Carolina was where Chiun was headed now. He wasn't going to the Caribbean with Remo. That would have been what Chiun perceived as being what Smith wanted.

If Remo knew Chiun, it would be a long time before Chiun was going to be cooperating with Smith. When the old man became offended, he stayed offended.

"I have to go to Haiti. I could use your help, Chiun."

"Why?"

"What do you mean, why? Who knows what I will run into there?"

"There will be nothing in Haiti that you will not be able to handle. Remember that you are the Reigning Master of Sinanju."

"I will remember that. But I'd like to have the Reigning Master of Sinanju Emeritus there, too."

"You'll not need me. Smith does not need me. I will be meditating."

"What say you fly down to Haiti with me first, then on the way back I'll drop you at the camper?"

"I am going to meditate at my home. The car will be here shortly to take me to the airport. You shall carry my chest to the car."

Remo paced to the front of the suite, then paced to the back. "Okay, so I probably won't need you in Haiti. It's just a bunch of religious nuts. The real problem is that it could be a while before I see you again, and I don't think we should leave each other without talking about this."

"Talking about what?"

"Your illness."

"I am not ill."

"You're a sick man."

Chiun was somber. "More insults. First from Harold the Mad, now from my own adopted son."

"I'm worried about you getting sick. That's not an insult."

"You imply a weakness in my constitution," Chiun said calmly. He was sitting cross-legged on the mat in their quarters at Folcroft Sanitarium, and had yet to open his eyes to Remo.

"Why can't we just get past the fact that you could be getting sick?" Remo demanded. "What's the big problem?"

"There is no problem. I am not sick," Chiun sniffed, and he rose gracefully and silently. Chiun stepped off the mat and swept it with his foot. The mat rolled itself into a perfect cylinder that traveled across the room and came to rest against one of Chiun's traveling trunks. He was returning home. Alone. Remo didn't like the idea of Chiun being alone, not when he might be ill.

"There are many things that you say about which I do not agree," Chiun said. "Many, many things. This is no different."

"It is different. It is important."

"To you."

"If it's important to me, shouldn't it be important to you just because it is important to me?" Remo said.

"No." Chiun touched the gleaming lock to a lacquered Asian trunk, and then lifted the lid. He took the mat and nestled it inside the trunk, then turned to Remo, tucking his hands into the sleeves of his robe.

"All right, Remo. Say what you wish to say."

"I don't wish to say anything, Little Father. I wish to talk about this with you. Back and forth. You then me. Conversation. About your sickness."

"There is no sickness. I am in perfect health."

"For a Master of Sinanju?"

"For any human being of any age, at any age, I am in superior health. Do you wish me to perform some acrobatic tricks to convince you?"

Remo twisted his unnaturally thick wrists. They were the only outward physical sign that there was something about him that was not normal. Other than the wrists, he looked like any other man you might see on the streets of any American city. Indeterminate in age, more or less slim, not too tall. Just some guy from Jersey in a pair of expensive Italian shoes, off-the-rack chinos and the kinds of shirts that came three to a package at the discount door.

"You know what, Chiun? I'm beginning to believe you about not feeling sick. You are as miserable an old bastard as you ever were."

"Remo!"

"And heartless and cold."

"That is uncalled for."

"You mean, inappropriate? You saying I've got bad manners?"

"Exactly."

"'Scuse me for caring. I'm going to Haiti." Remo tried to slam the door behind him, but Chiun slipped up and eased it shut.

When the car came to pick him up sometime later, Chiun was forced to carry his own luggage.

8

Remo Williams passed the time moodily adding up the number of sleazy little Caribbean seaside towns he'd seen, but gave up. It was a depressing exercise.

He remembered watching a silly pirate movie that had the swashbucklers visiting a Caribbean town two hundred years ago, supposedly filthy, supposedly with swine and human beings sleeping in the muddy gutters. On screen, it all looked way too clean compared to the reality Remo knew.

Hawkers swarmed the new arrivals as soon as they exited the chain-link pen that served as the airport in the southwestern coastal town in the Dominican Republic. A teenager in relief-agency blue jeans jerked his head conspiratorially at Remo. "What choo need?"

"Not a thing, thanks."

"I got whatever you need. Panel trucks. Wholesale rum by the case. Loading crews. You name it."

"Aren't you supposed to be selling wacky weed?"

The kid's face twitched. "I can get you whatever you want. You want that stuff, you can get it. As for me, there ain't no money in it. I would rather rent you a pickup truck."

"Are you the official Hertz representative in this city?"

"Well, what I mean is this, I can sell you a pickup truck, temporarily. I can even stock it for you."

"Why would I want a pickup truck?"

The kid slit his eyes as if trying to read Remo Williams. Maybe he looked in the American's eyes for the first time and realized he was dealing with someone who was not your ordinary transient American. The kid didn't like what he saw. He skipped up the smelly street, then made a quick dive into the nearest dark doorway.

Remo didn't know what to make of the encounter until he had a second one. The comely young woman wore a carefully distressed white blouse, threadbare in the most eye-catching places, and jeans cut off to mid-buttock. She approached Remo with a secret smile.

"Hi."

"It is a beautiful day, miss, " Remo said suspiciously.

"To think I got something you want."

"Uh-huh. Which is what?" He eyed her see-through blouse warily.

"Ford Excursion, all-wheel-drive, with a full tank of gas and all the seats removed. Very spacious interior."

"And what are you offering to do in the Ford Excursion with all the seats removed?"

"What I will do is give you the key and let you drive away in it. Now, let's talk inventory."

"Okay. Talk."

"I can supply vodka, whiskey, rum. Generic brands in plastic bottles to save on weight. I can sell you forty cases. I'll have it loaded for you."

"That is an awful lot of alcohol, and the truth is, miss, I'm not much of a drinking man."

"You don't need to be. All you need to be is a man who wants to get rich."

"Well, now, that's a real noggin scratcher. How, exactly, would I get rich?"

The young woman sighed. "You're going to the Priestess's village, right? All Americans who come here now are on their way to the village. All of them are going to a new life. But that doesn't mean you can't be rich when you get there. And the one thing they don't have in the village is drink. They got sex, they got food and they got everything you could want, except drink. And you go in there with a truck full of drink, you can finance yourself for months."

To Remo this made a weird kind of sense.

"Thanks, but no thanks. So why do they call it the Church of Remo, anyway?"

The girl looked at him strangely. "How should I know? I am Dominican. You are American. I would think you would know."

"Seems like really weird name for a religion."

"It makes no sense to me. Doesn't it means something in American?"

"I really need to know the answer," Remo said. "In fact, once I know the answer, I can probably go home."

"If I come up with the answer for you, how much you pay?"

Remo shook his head. "Forget it."

She walked away, but Remo called. "Hey, what about a phone?"

"You want a phone in the Ford? I'll throw it in for free. We have a deal?"

"No, I mean a public phone. Where's one I can use?"

She pointed up the street. "Two blocks." She walked away without further clarification.

Remo strolled up the street, obviously a main street in the town. He wondered how cities in the tropical islands could somehow manage to be totally lifeless when surrounded by a wealth of greenery. How hard was it to bring a few plants in from the suburbs? He wondered how he was supposed to spot the telephone when all he knew was "two blocks" in a certain direction.

Then he saw the obvious place for a telephone.

WHEN HAROLD W. SMITH took the call, he heard what seemed to be the voice of Remo Williams saying, "Big Bad Bunch of Fries is one dollar and sixty-five cents American. Big Bad Bacon Burger—that's the one with extra *extra* bacon—two dollars and sixteen cents, American."

"Remo? What are you doing?"

"Hey, Smitty. I was telling the fake Sarah about fast-food prices down here in paradise."

"What fake Sarah?"

"The computer voices on the screening system. They all sound just like Sarah these days."

"I do not think so, Remo."

"I do think so, Smitty. I'm the one who listens to them all the time so I ought to know. I think Mark is programming his girlfriend in, as a way of showing his devotion."

"Mark would never do anything so careless."

"I'm telling you, Smitty. They are all Sarah these days. This one was a kindergarten schoolteacher in Anchorage, and when I told her I was calling from the Dominican Republic, she wanted to know what it was like down there. She's never been out of Alaska. So I was telling her that the prices on fast food are a good twenty percent cheaper, although I bet it tastes exactly the same. It sure stinks the same."

Harold W. Smith examined the window on his desktop screen, which revealed the location of the incoming call. "You are phoning from a Muck-Mickey's fast-food establishment in Pedernales."

"Yes, I thought we had established that," Remo said. "You know, I was propositioned twice in ten minutes by unsavory characters wanting to rent me a truck. I've traveled some, and I've rented cars all over the world. But I never had an offer like this before. They wanted to fill it up with cases of booze for me."

"You do not drink, Remo," Smith said.

"True enough, Smitty," Remo said. "I don't think they wanted to sell me booze for personal consumption. I think they were trying to provide me with inventory to sell at the village."

"I see."

Remo was listening to Harold Smith in his office overlooking Long Island Sound in Rye, New York, tapping on his keys. Smith didn't seem to care about the propositions. "I'll see if I can get a seat on one of the shuttle buses going over to the village."

"Are you saying that these locals were offering to sell you the vehicle and stock it for you with alcohol, to be sold in the village when you arrived?"

"That was the business plan."

"And the intention was for you to pay in cash, then keep all the proceeds of the village sale?"

"That's it. So why?"

"There is something strange about the setup. If it was a money-making venture as lucrative as they make it sound, why not do their own shipping and selling of the merchandise?"

"How should I know?"

"I'd like to find out. Maybe it will give us a glimpse of the underside of the Church of Remo."

"I hate this kind of snooping spying stuff," Remo said. "Hold on. Let me get it over with."

He dropped the phone and jogged away from the burger mart, and he could hear Smith calling, "Remo? Are you there?"

Remo moved up the street until he found a familiar face. Remo caught up to her on a street corner, where she had one hip cocked provocatively at the traffic.

"I decided I'd like a little more information about your car rental agreement," Remo said. "What exactly is the cost to me to purchase an SUV, including taxes and optional collision damage insurance?"

"That will cost you ten thousand American, American," the young woman said, looking impatient. She thought Remo was wasting her time.

Remo nodded. "I see. And how much would it cost me for the cases of generic, plastic bottles of booze? A full load?"

"That's five thousand dollars."

Remo's eyes rolled up into his head as the numbers fought to come to some sort of conclusion in his brain. Math had never been a strong point.

"Seems like an awful lot for the booze, and not too much for the truck."

"That truck, it is not much of a truck. It's been around awhile. I give you the guarantee you'll get where you are going. After that you don't need it anyway, right?"

"I guess so," Remo said.

"Later, we'll come and probably want to buy it back from you for a fair price. Then the booze," the girl continued, moving her shoulders back to stress the failing threads of her blouse. "You can resell the alcohol when you get there for a thousand percent markup."

Remo nodded seriously. "I see. Then I assume that I can more than recoup my investment in the truck."

"Of course you can."

Remo nodded, trying to figure out how much money he would make off the booze and if, in fact, the profits were there.

Not that it mattered. He didn't see himself going into the hard-liquor-distribution business. "Now, what I'm wondering is this. If it's so easy to make a lot of money by selling hooch to the villagers at the Priestess's place, why aren't you doing it?"

The working girl made a sour face. "That," she said, "is a fair question. The answer is that I am Dominican. There are difficulties set up for me going into Haiti. White Americans have no problem going in. Dominicans on business—no."

"Is there some sort of an electric fence and military guards or something?"

"This is not like the United States border with Canada. This is Hispaniola. There are impromptu checkpoints. They do not dare to touch Americans. Dominicans they can touch, no problem. There is much invisible protection for you in this country and in Haiti."

Remo thought it all made good sense. "So what exactly are you not telling me?"

She never lost her streetwalker smile. "There is nothing that I'm not telling you."

"There is something. It all seems a little too easy."

Remo could read her little lie. He could see it in

the shifting of her eyes and the faint acceleration of her pulse and in the tiny catches in her breathing. These were the telltale signs of deceit that almost no human being could even sense, let alone decipher. Remo could sense the signs, and knew what they meant. She wasn't giving him the *whole* truth. He leaned closer and placed a gentle hand on her elbow.

She made no sound, but her eyes opened a little more. Inside, she was screaming.

"I think you better give me all the fine print," Remo suggested.

He released her elbow, then she begged, "Please don't do that to me again."

"I hope not to."

She tried to run away, but Remo caught hold of her again. "All I want is to know what you are not telling me."

She was smarter than most of the people whom Remo Williams got hold of. It only took her one reminder to convince her that she really should just come clean. She did.

Remo jogged back up the street to the fast-food place and found the manager on the pay phone.

"You stop calling here!" He slammed down the receiver, and the phone began ringing again almost at once. In a rage, the manager snatched the receiver and began beating it against the phone box.

"I'll take that," Remo said, taking the receiver from the manager's hands.

"You cannot use it. There is this man who keeps calling. He will not get off. And the phone will not work for other patrons."

"It is okay."

"You know this man?" the manager demanded.

"I'll get rid of him for you," Remo said. Then he spoke into the phone, "Hiya, Smitty."

"Remo," Smith said, his voice as sour as a man sucking bad fruit. "I will not speak to you with that man there."

The manager had turned his wrath on Remo and was giving him a piece of his mind in a Dominican dialect that made no sense to Remo. Remo patted the man on the back and targeted his fingertips into the soft part of his spinal column, and the manager became stiff and quiet. The manager of the restaurant was confused, but not in pain—simply unable to make any sound come from his mouth. In fact, his face was frozen, his jaw stuck open, and he brought his hands to his head to find out why. As his fear grew, Remo gave him a gentle shove toward the counter. The manager of the franchise began pantomiming at the counter for the benefit of his pitying employees.

Soon there was chaos behind the counter. Someone was calling for an ambulance. Someone else was wrapping a dishrag on the manager's face and trying to tighten it to force his mouth closed.

"Okay, we're all alone," Remo said.

"So what's all the shouting?" Smith asked.

"That's just business as usual here in the Dominican Republic." Remo explained the booze-selling scheme. The Dominicans could not get into Haiti without a hassle. Americans could get in without being molested simply because they were Americans.

"They claim that the Americans are pretty much untouchable, with protection by the American government and by the Priestess herself. The Haitians won't touch an American after they are a part of the village."

"That seems unlikely. As far as we know, the Priestess has no enforcement staff."

"So how does she keep the peace?"

"Unknown. Maybe she'd just keeps her worshipers satisfied, and there's no need for law enforcement."

"Well, there's a little bit more to the story," Remo said. "The Priestess doesn't like even her own people bringing booze into the village. There are stories about even the villagers getting reprimanded for selling booze to other religions. Reprimanded by the Priestess."

"How reprimanded?" Smith asked.

"Nobody knows, " Remo said mysteriously. "At least, my little car prostitute didn't know. Why does any of this matter?"

"It doesn't," Smith said.

9

Remo got out of the car again. "What's that thing?" He jabbed a finger at the dashboard.

"Gearshift."

"No. That."

"Telephone."

Remo glowered. "You didn't say anything about a telephone. Does it work?"

"Sure, if you buy the phone service."

"Can you show me how to turn it off?"

The kid had the feeling that neither of them was fully communicating with the other. "The phone won't work if you haven't bought a service," he explained again.

"I don't want it working at all."

"But it won't work."

"Then turn it off."

"It's hard-wired into the car. I don't know how to turn it off."

"Then break it," Remo said.

"Why?"

"Humor me."

"I don't wish to break it. What if the car comes back to us?"

"Hey, I bought this car, right? I own it fair and square," Remo said. "I want the telephone broken."

"Then you can do the breaking of it yourself," the kid said angrily. He didn't know what he was even arguing about.

"I can't break it," Remo complained. "I'll end up frying the whole car's electric system or something."

The kid shrugged and eagerly ended the conversation.

Remo was driving less than ten minutes before the phone rang.

"Son of a bitch." He poked the talk button and assumed the phone would instantly become nonfunctional. It was the effect he had on electronic devices. Anything computerized tended to go through a catastrophic failure anytime he placed his fingers on it.

The trouble was, everything was electronic these days. Electric toothbrushes, home pregnancy tests, rental cars. Remo could still find the old manual toothbrushes, and he seldom had need for pregnancy tests, but he was always renting cars. More and more, the controls baffled and annoyed him—and often ceased to work as soon as he touched them.

No such luck on this occasion. The phone continued to work perfectly as the little display announced the incoming call was connected.

"Ola?"

"Remo, it's me." It was an old man, voice so sour he sounded as if he had a mouthful of lemons. Harold W. Smith.

"No Remo. Horhe."

"Is this supposed to be entertaining or deceptive, Remo?"

"No habla ingles."

"You speak Spanish even worse," Smith said. "It's fortuitous that you happened to rent a car with a phone."

"Fortuitous is not the F-word I'd use," Remo said. "How'd you find me so fast?"

"Your purchase of the car was made on a credit card. I traced that to the car records and found the serial number of its phone. I've activated an account on the phone for you. You neglected to do so when you purchased it."

"Slipped my mind. So why are you calling?"

"Just checking in," Smith said. "It is somewhat of a novelty, to be honest, since you are so frequently incommunicado."

"You do sound giddy as a schoolgirl," Remo said, although Harold Smith had never, ever sounded giddy in his life.

"It is becoming easier all the time to keep in touch with you in the field, Remo, despite your persistent refusal to carry a phone."

"I noticed," Remo said dismally.

"It may be time for you to finally give up your childish stubbornness on this point."

"We tried it, remember?" Remo said. "Several times. It doesn't work. The phones get broken."

"There are satellite phones available now that are built for battlefield operations. They're constructed to endure extreme conditions, and they're smaller than the phones you've used in the past."

"Are you trying to telemarket me?" Remo demanded. "So where do I go?"

"The village of the Priestess is in the Mangrove Preserves. It is the South Coastal Haitian Environmental and Erosion Prevention Preserve. It's a national park."

"Haiti has national parks?" Remo asked.

"They better. It's the only thing keeping the south coast from washing into the ocean every time there's a tropical storm."

"Oh, now I understand," Remo lied.

"You'll be in the preserve in under an hour."

"I heard it is the Haitian National Swamp."

"Not a swamp," Smith said. "It's the south coastal mangrove preserve. It's one of the last old-growth mangrove forests on the south cost of Haiti. The U.S. has spent millions to plant more mangroves and expand the forest."

"Why the U.S.?" Remo asked.

"The U.S. has largely been paying the bills for Haitian cleanup efforts from years of tropical storms that have torn up Haiti. The country has been deforested so heavily that there's no natural protection from mudslides and floods when the storms hit."

"So? Doesn't explain why the U.S. is paying to plant a swamp in Haiti."

"Less expensive in the long run," Smith said. "The more forests are restored, the less erosion and more stability when the next hurricane hits. The old-growth mangrove forests are being surrounded by thousands of acres of new plantings. The U.S. has a permanent military presence in the area. Their job is to keep the Haitians from cutting down the new growth. You'll pass through a checkpoint at the border of the preserve."

"Wait. The cult village is in the national park? How come that's allowed?"

"They grandfathered in," Smith said. "The Priestess's corporation bought a high-ground estate inside the old-growth forest. The government had forgotten the property was even there. But the Priestess found the family who held legal title and gave them what had to be a small fortune to a Haitian. She's the legal owner now. The environmentalists were not happy. They've put observers all around the village to watch for signs of environmental damage. They're looking for an excuse to have the Priestess and her flock evicted."

"Sounds like an easy answer to the problem. Theirs and ours."

"Except the village has committed no known violations of the environmental rules of the preserve," Smith said. "In addition, the observers have all joined the flock."

"Seems like everybody who visits the place ends up staying," Remo said. "What if I decide to retire to the village?"

Smith said with dead seriousness, "You may not. You have time left on your contract."

"Yeah, but you know what a shrewd negotiator I am, Smitty."

Smith said, "I know you came to the last round of contract renegotiations with your notes scribbled on the back of a shipping receipt."

"Whatever works," Remo said. "Nice chatting with you."

Remo pressed the Off button on the dashboard.

"That's why I don't carry a phone, you old grouch," he grumbled.

"Duly noted," said Smith from the dashboard, and then there was a click.

10

Joey Wild felt as if he were getting called to the principal's office, but he had never been so terrified of any principal in school. Then again, the assistant deans at his high school were not quite as freaky as the Priestess's bodyguards, or whatever they were.

Joey had seen a couple of them around the village and asked about them, and people had been uninterested or uneasy about the strange men who hung around the Priestess.

Some said there were as many as a dozen of them. Some said there were only five or six. Only one of them had a name that anybody knew, and he was the only one of the bunch who seemed anywhere near normal. He was Todd Rohrman, a skinny, light-in-the-loafers type, who always seemed brittle and agitated and on the verge of a freak-out. The others all had strangely dark gray complexions and hardened faces, but the strangest looking of them all was the one who came for Joey Wild—he was nicknamed Leatherhead in the village.

His skin looked like old, water-damaged leather—like the shell of a thirty-year-old football somebody found in their attic. Joey heard that Leatherhead must have been in some kind of an accident, but when Joey got close to the man he could see that the condition was too consistent on the flesh covering his entire body. As if he had been born with this skin condition. Leatherhead walked around in the uniform of the poor Haitians, like the other dark-skinned acolytes. They were ancient, brown trousers and shirts and ancient sandals.

Wild got his close, firsthand look at Leatherhead when Leatherhead appeared at the door of his little studio condominium. Wild had just returned from the pleasure pavilions for a quick shower before heading off to the noon feast.

Leatherhead said nothing, and the silence was unbearable.

"Well? What do you need?" Wild asked.

Leatherhead said nothing, but crossed one arm in front of them and pointed toward the century-old stone remains of what had been a rich Haitian's mansion once upon a time. That was the home of the Priestess.

Few had ever heard any of the Priestess's acolytes

speak, but the rumor was they could speak. Wild considered the man obstinate, but he couldn't think of any good reason for being uncooperative. Instead he shook his head and said, "Okay, let's go."

Wild started down the stone path through the middle village, Leatherhead falling behind him, silent except for his feet scraping on the path. Wild was embarrassed. The people were stopping what they were doing to watch the procession. It was an unusual sight. Wild himself had never seen anyone paraded through the village in this fashion.

He didn't know what to expect. His fear mounted, and he forgot the people of the village.

Above all, he felt confused, even betrayed. He had fallen easily into the carefree lifestyle of the village, living it up, partaking of the pleasures, even dancing at the ceremonial bonfires. This was the way his life was meant to be. It was unfair that stress and worry had been brought back into it.

Challenge and purpose were highly overrated. What little ambition there was in his character was easily satisfied by the occasional afternoon of booze selling. His accidental taste of the liquor-distribution business had become a thriving little enterprise.

He would call his suppliers in Pedernales up the coast and learn when the next shipment of village newcomers was scheduled. The new male arrivals would often come individually, while the females always came in gaggles.

The women would have a heavy load of inhibitions when they arrived, and were always reluctant to release themselves to the pleasures of the village until they had gone through the initiating ceremonies that the Priestess held for them. It was just another bonfire, drinking the unpleasant ceremonial island tea, but somehow the tea acted as a symbolic release of the will to the pleasures of the Priestess. Once they went through the initiation, the women opened up.

The men were different. They arrived with their mind already open, ready to leap into the extracurricular activities.

The open mind started before they even reached the village. It was easy to convince them that they would be doing the village a favor by driving in a shipment of supplies—for a modest fee.

His contacts in Pedernales no longer had to take a steep cut on the business. By working with Joey Wild, the Pedernales business made more money, Joey Wild made more money and the new arrivals were thrilled to have helped out the cause, so long as they got to sample the pleasure pavilions right away.

There had been instances in which the liquor was

confiscated by the acolytes of the Priestess on the village outskirts. Sometimes the new arrivals got angry at being embroiled in trouble as soon as they arrived, or so Joey Wild heard. Sometimes they even complained to the Priestess about being tricked in Pedernales. Had this trouble been linked back to Joey Wild? Probably.

But why was there so much resistance to booze? It was all over the village anyway. The Priestess supposedly didn't even care that there was booze on her land, so long as it was kept out of sight. The unofficial rules of the village stated that alcohol was okay so long as you kept it discreet. Everybody understood that.

Joey Wild had come to monopolize the village alcohol distribution in a matter of days. It was easy, since there was essentially no one else in the business, just a succession of one-off distributors. Through his phone contacts, he organized the deliveries and standardized prices. Everybody benefited.

He was performing a valuable service. He gave the people what they wanted, he kept it low-profile for the Priestess and he wasn't ripping anybody off.

But he wondered if the Priestess would see things the way he did.

He decided there were two possible outcomes.

She would either see him as a troublemaker or an asset. Maybe he should be ready to plead his case and offer to give her a cut. He began to visualize a spreadsheet of his profits and losses and mentally calculate his profits based on giving a ten percent cut to the Priestess. Maybe twenty percent, tops.

Hell, it worked out to be a sweet deal for him, even if he gave her fifty percent. The booze was cheap, the work was easy and Wild didn't have any place to spend his money anyway. It all went into his account at the U.S. bank branch at Pedernales. Everything he needed was provided for by the Priestess.

What if she told him to either stop selling his booze or to leave the village forever?

What would he do then?

Joey Wild began to tremble. He couldn't leave here. He had seen the light. It was at the initiation dance on his first night, where he drank the ceremonial tea. This was the symbolic binding of the worshiper to the Priestess. It was the one and only time she had spoken to him—and he didn't even remember what she had said.

"Drink this," she'd instructed.

He'd drunk. All the village had watched. She'd bent and whispered in his ear.

She was indescribably beautiful. Maybe her mere

presence kept him from hearing her message, but from that moment forward, Joey Wild was madly determined to be in the village, to give all he could to the Priestess.

Besides, he really was enjoying himself in the village. It had lived up to its reputation. The food was plentiful, free and tasty. The accommodations were good enough, when he considered that he spent almost all his time outside his little studio condominium socializing and cavorting.

Joey Wild had been in the village a short while and he knew that eventually he would get tired of the simple pleasure it offered. Someday. Like when he was ninety. He'd worry about it when it happened.

They came to the old Haitian mortared-stone wall that served as the front entrance to the Priestess's compound. The first wide arc opened into the semi-private courtyard. The villagers could see into this place as they went about their business. Beyond it was a double wooden door in another stone gate, leading to the secluded retreat beyond.

This was the private domain of the Priestess. When she appeared to her flock, she emerged from her home to do so. Even when she met with her people casually, she would at least come out into her courtyard to talk. No one entered through the double doors into the private sanctuary.

But now Leatherhead marched Joey Wild to the double doors and waved at them.

Joey Wild went in.

THE OPEN, circular courtyard inside the archway was paved with old time-worn flagstones set in the earth with a few plants along the edges. The walkway continued to another set of double doors, which entered the stone mansion itself.

Leatherhead closed the doors behind them, and Joey Wild was locked inside the Priestess's courtyard.

As far as Joey Wild had heard, no one had ever seen inside the Priestess's private hideaway, and no one knew what her mansion even looked like. He was the first one to be here. Was it an honor or was it ominous?

The courtyard itself was pleasant, cool, verdant, even if it was walled in by a ten-foot stone wall. If Joey Wild was a prisoner, it did not seem like a high-security prison. He could get over that wall easily enough by clambering up a stone bench to an overhanging mangrove branch.

But he wasn't going to need to escape. For crying out loud, they weren't going to *hurt* him. The worst that could happen was that he'd be banished from the village.

The building opened and there was Todd Rohrman, the one normal-looking acolyte of the Priestess. His face was drawn and his limbs were wiry. The interest he showed in Wild was the interest of a police officer checking out a suspicious-looking character in front of the convenience store.

Rohrman looked beyond Wild, and Wild was startled to realize there were people there. The double doors had never opened, so how did they get there? They were the acolytes, of course, and, close-up, Wild could see how very different they all looked from Todd Rohrman. He wasn't one of them. They weren't like him. They weren't quite like anything Wild knew of. They were all brown, tough skin and oily black hair and brown, dull eyes that had no life in them.

There was the one called Leatherhead at the head of the pack.

Next came Jar Carrier—that was his nickname in the village, anyway. He looked like someone's grandfather, who once had been very tall but whose body was collapsing from the weight of his own skeleton and hunched like a rat gnawing on a seed. His tanned flesh was cracked and dry, except around his eyes, which glistened with a pungent grease. It was as if he had spread a generous smear of lard from one temple to the other, right over his eyes.

Around his neck on a leather cord was a small clay pot with a carved wooden stopper, tied in place with more leather cords. The jar was smeared with the same grease.

The next acolyte was known as Sandal Wearer, or by other, less kind names, in the village. He wore just a pair of worn, faded britches, held on his hips by a belt of braided leather. Unlike the other acolytes, this one had something on his feet. A huge pair of sandals, for what must have been size nineteen feet. The sandals looked as if they should be in a Pioneer Days museum.

The next acolyte wore a shirt, as well as trousers, making him look almost overdressed. He held his shoulders pulled back as if unable to relax them, and his head seemed to be misshapen, as if he had been in an accident that had deformed it. His nose was crooked from multiple breaks and his cheeks seemed to have been smashed flat. He was the Drunkard, but he wasn't really a drunk. They simply called him that in the village because he was prone to suddenly collapse without reason for minutes or an hour at a time. He seemed to enjoy startling the people in the village by grinning at them maliciously then collapsing violently to the earth. Wild had seen him do it. He could swear the man had his fits deliberately, and didn't care about getting his face damaged in the falls.

There was at least one more acolyte, but he was missing at the moment. Treetop Man was always seen climbing in the trees like an old, hideous chimp.

Todd Rohrman should have felt some affinity for Joey Wild. After all, they were the two normals in a garden of freaks. But Rohrman was impatient, and after a wordless moment of waiting he turned away from them all, strolled to the edge of a tinkling, bathtub-size fountain and rested his buttocks on the stone ledge.

Rohrman's movement attracted the attention of Jar Carrier, who rotated his head like a bird to follow Rohrman's movements, fascinated. He continued to watch the man sit on the stone fountain ledge and trail his fingers in the water of the pool. Joey Wild had thought to get chummy with Rohrman, but clearly the man had no interest in him socially. So Wild just stood there. This seemed to be what was expected of him.

It seemed to be what was expected of all of them. After some minutes, Wild cleared his throat. Jar Carrier's head snapped in his direction. Jar Carrier jerked his head and examined him intently, as if trying to figure out what in the world Joey Wild had just done. Wild was embarrassed for some reason.

The last thing that Joey Wild expected to hear then was giggling, but the front of the Priestess's mansion opened up and gigglers emerged. They were a half dozen women, and Wild recognized them as the females from the latest arriving group. Wild had assessed them as a reticent, somber bunch when they'd gotten off the shuttle bus. The women had clung to their male counterparts and there was an urgent group discussion right outside the doors of the bus, and it had looked as if they were getting ready climb back in to go back to where they had come from.

That was when he had seen Todd Rohrman show up, in a clean outfit and with his most engaging smile. His hair had looked blow-dried. He'd looked as if he was wearing makeup. The young man had struck up an instant, nonthreatening rapport with the women. He'd invited them somewhere while the men settled in—then the women were lured to one of the pleasure pavilions, after which they needed no more convincing.

Wild had watched the tension melt from the group as the ladies went off with Todd and the men went to find their accommodations. It seemed to be standard operating procedure, used to make new and nervous female arrivals feel at home. And it worked. The women were always convinced to stay.

Nobody ever left the village, because nobody ever wanted to leave the village. Nothing sinister about that. It was simply the inexorable, intransigent truth.

The Priestess came as soon as the women left the private courtyard. Joey Wild had seen the Priestess at the evening ceremonies, but he had never been able to really look at her. She was exquisite, but even that was far too plain a word to describe the Priestess. She was many things, all of them attractive and appealing. The giggling girlishness of her chat with the woman was melting from her face, leaving almost emptiness, and she concentrated on Joey Wild.

She almost seemed intoxicated.

"Who are you?"

"Joseph Wild, Priestess."

"You're not him."

"Priestess, this is the liquor dealer," Rohrman said, coming to her side.

The Priestess turned on Rohrman and considered it, and Wild thought she had the behavior of an old woman, slow-moving, partially deaf.

"Ah," she said.

"How are you Priestess?" Rohrman said.

"I'm fine," she answered. "Where is the other?"

"Patrolling," he said.

They both glanced at the mangrove trees. The Priestess was listening, waiting for something to happen, then asked Wild, "Who is this?"

Rohrman frowned. "This is the liquor dealer."

"He's not the one I want!"

"You asked us to bring him here, Priestess. This morning at breakfast. Don't you even remember, Minister?"

Her head snapped up, her eyes became sparkling clear and lucid for the first time, and to Wild's astonishment she lashed out at Rohrman with a hard sucker jab to the soft, fleshy intersection of his collarbones. "Don't call me that!"

Rohrman choked. "Yes, Priestess."

The flashing in her eyes seemed to cloud and the stiffness left her posture, and she turned away. Then she was gone. The freaks never made a move. Joey Wild didn't know exactly what to do next.

"Get out," Rohrman said. "Just send him back."

Rohrman was distressed. Joey Wild was wondering if he had just been saved from something more than a talking to. And whatever was wrong with his precious Priestess? He didn't think he should ask Rohrman. Rohrman seemed to be the boss when the Priestess wasn't around. The scrawny fruitcake seemed to have quite a power base.

"Consider yourself lucky," Rohrman added as Wild left.

"I do," Wild said with perfect sincerity. "We all do."

11

Joey Wild was at a loss. He didn't have his television to give him direction. He didn't know how to make his next life-altering decision. Without television, without a damn radio, how was he supposed to know which path to take? How was he supposed to find guidance?

Should he opt for the path of least resistance, and quit the booze business? Or should he take steps to make himself rich, and keep the liquor flowing at the village?

His meeting with the Priestess couldn't have been less conclusive.

He needed a sign from heaven, or the nearest electronic video device. Or a substitute electronic device.

But there were few electronic devices in the village. Who needed them?

Wild still had his cell phone. As he strode back

to his condo he found the phone in his khaki shorts—his only garb these days—and flipped through its functions. He didn't get much of a signal out here, but it was enough to call his business partners in Pedernales from time to time. How could he use the phone to elicit a message from the Fates? Call information?

He could try some text messaging. But whom would he text message? It was the same problem. He could download a cheesy video game or thumb through his electronic planner, looking for some sort of random message.

There had to be some way to make the telephone display random messages that could contain Wild's hidden, intrinsic meaning. Alarm clock? Useless. He kept pressing buttons helplessly, ignoring the daily life in the village around him. He had a hundred pointless functions in the little aluminum device and they were all useless—until he came upon an unfamiliar image. The two-inch screen displayed a clearing, in a mangrove forest. A man was on the ground doing some sort of performance art.

It was the camera function. Joey had forgotten he even had one on the phone. It was showing him exactly what was happening in front of him at this moment. When Joey looked up, he saw that his old friend Lance Belmont was the man doing the artistic performing.

Lance contorted, then got to his feet and danced. Lance was really getting into the act, which was a lot like the dancing they did at the blurry evening ceremonials.

No, it was no act. Lance was in distress. His eyes were bloodred. He got back on the ground to continue gyrating, and one of the village residents came to his side, bringing another villager who was a former doctor.

Joey Wild watched, fascinated, through the display screen on his camera phone as he experienced enlightenment.

He had asked for a sign and this closest thing to the television set was giving him a sign. He just didn't know what this sign meant—yet.

The doctor lifted up a little plastic bottle and sniffed it.

"Rubbing alcohol," the doctor said sadly. "The poor fool's drinking whatever he can get his hands on. Doesn't he know this stuff can kill you?"

"Will it kill him?" one of the other village residents asked.

Joey Wild was startled by the concept of Lance Belmont becoming dead from his own addiction. Why didn't the poor guy just leave the village if he needed to drink so badly?

The answer—because nobody ever left the village. Leaving was unthinkable. *Nothing* was worth the anguish of leaving the village.

But the village of the Priestess was a place of peace, serenity and protection from all that was wrong and terrible in the world. The Priestess assured them of this. But here was an ugly reminder of the outside world right in front of them.

Something was wrong, Wild thought. Lance wouldn't be drinking rubbing alcohol if I'd taken my delivery yesterday.

Watching the doctor administer some sort of injection into Lance's arm was not giving Wild his answers, but when he turned back to the little phone screen and saw the same events displayed electronically, they made sense. It was a neatly contained scene, uncluttered by extraneous information, and it allowed Wild's answers to present themselves.

This was the reason the Priestess had summoned him this morning. The rancor of the acolytes was no concern. He must concentrate only on what the Priestess was communicating to him. She was almost oblivious to him once he was at the meeting. So why had he been summoned? To put him in this place at the right time, after the meeting! It could not be a coincidence.

Joey Wild understood. In some way, he was responsible for Lance Belmont.

Joey looked at his meeting with a fresh perspective. The Priestess's feigned confusion was a message disguised as a symbol. She was telling him that she didn't understand his actions. She didn't know why he had ceased providing a needed service to the village. When she said he was not the one she wanted, the Priestess was allegorically illustrating that Joey was not the man he should be—the benevolent safe keeper of the village alcoholics.

He got it. He must continue his holy work. She said so—she had sanctioned his liquor-distribution business, if only to protect the members of her flock from the same fate as poor Lance Belmont.

Joey closed the phone and it rang, not a minute later. It was one of his business partners in Pedernales.

"What's your status, friend?" his provider asked.

"Ready to do more business. I don't think we should expect any more trouble."

"Is that so? You got yourself a little protection?"

"More or less. You could call it official sanctioning. I have the blessing of the Priestess herself."

"Is that so?"

"When can you send a shipment?"

"I can do it now. Give me fifteen minutes to get the boxes in the back and round up the driver. You can expect to take delivery by midafternoon."

JOEY WILD FOUND himself whistling. Everything would work out fine. His good buddy Lance seemed to be coming around. He was on his hands and knees, hacking up the poison. He'd be just fine.

When he turned to head back to his little condo, Wild found himself face-to-face with Leatherhead, standing there silent and just staring at him.

Joey Wild gave the freak a mock salute. "Message received. Loud and clear. Thanks for you help."

Leatherhead didn't smile or change his expression in any way, but Joey Wild could tell the freak was pleased that Wild had understood the intent of his mistress.

IT WAS A GOOD DAY for Joey Wild. The liquor came in on schedule. He paid his cash and opened his impromptu liquor store a few yards outside the village limits. As he briskly sold off the merchandise, he kept a running profit-and-loss spreadsheet in his head. Any company on the planet would be thrilled to have a balance sheet like his. He was making something on the order of eighty percent profit on every deal. He had more money than he could possibly ever use in a lifetime at the village.

Lance Belmont managed to get to the sale before

the inventory was bought out. He was barely able to walk, but he made it.

"There's my trouper! How you feeling, buddy?" Joey asked.

"Shitty."

"What'd the doctor have to say?"

"Said I'm lucky I'm not dead. Said I'm lucky I don't have brain damage. Brain damage would be better than how I feel right now. I need some medicine to clean out the poison."

"You should know better than to drink that crap."

"No shit, Sherlock. I wasn't thinking. I was crazy or something." He plunked down a twenty-dollar bill. "Give me something to make me sane."

12

Todd Rohrman felt as if he spent his every waking minute feeling nauseous.

It hadn't always been this way. Once he had been healthy, happy and gay, living a thrilling, debauched lifestyle in the capital town of Union Island. He'd had had a great job, a fashion-conscious boss and all kinds of prospects for the future. He'd had a nice little power base, too—not enough to be a bother, but just enough to keep him hopping. The island's revolving door of tourism kept him supplied with plenty of playmates. They were always impressed by Rohrman's VIP status among the island's upper crust and *always* their vacations ended before their company became stale or turned tiresome.

He had been assistant to the minister of tourism. She was a treasure. All girl, with hips and hair and all that, and boobies that sent the hetero boys into fits. Fits! She knew how to use them, too—the boobies and the hair and all of it. She had the island president wrapped around her little finger. She was a bullet train of ambition, and Todd Rohrman had plans to ride her cute caboose all the way to the top. Someday she'd be the leader of Union Island. She'd do away with her chubby hubby, the former island president, show she could do so much better!

But Dawn Summens and Todd Rohrman were much alike in that neither of them liked to hang on to any one romantic boy-toy for too long. Rohrman knew then that he—yes, he—would always be the most important man in Dawn Summens's life.

He never dreamed he'd be the most important man in her death, as well.

What Todd Rohrman had never realized was that his precious minister of tourism was prone to fits of insanity.

She risked her career, and his, on wild schemes that Rohrman still didn't understand. It all had something to do with plotting against the island president. It was a poorly thought-out plan, and Rohrman still couldn't figure out what the whole point was. In the end, it was some sort of zombie nightmare on the streets of Union Island. Rohrman saw the mayhem in the streets and just said to hell with it. He took a bottle of sparkling wine to bed and slept through the night.

When he awoke with a bad headache, lots of people were dead, the president was missing and presumed dead. The Union Island government was being dismantled by the Feds, who were suddenly very interested in the paperwork of the Union Island bureaucracy. Todd Rohrman was investigated and cleared of wrongdoing, but he was out of a job.

What was worse was the death of his boss. He couldn't make himself go to her funeral. He couldn't tolerate seeing her in the pancake makeup of the funeral parlor. He even briefly considered stealing the body to do her face himself—then found out there wasn't going to be a funeral at all. She was being processed into the ground along with all the other dead locals.

He would have taken off for the mainland had he not still been under investigation, and it was a good thing he'd stayed on the island for a couple of days.

Because Dawn Summens rose from the grave, and her first stop was Todd Rohrman's apartment.

When she knocked on his door at three in the morning, when he stumbled to the door and opened it, when he saw her standing there, Todd Rohrman fainted dead away like some wide-eyed heroine from the silent pictures of a hundred years ago.

He came to and gave her a sandwich, then put her in the tub and washed her up. She didn't seem interested in the news from the island. She seemed to be thinking in strange ways. Who wouldn't? You wake up, find yourself buried alive, and you scratch yourself out of the grave. Not many people could have done it. Dawn Summens wasn't like many people.

She had to get off the island, she insisted. No hospital. She told her plans to Todd, and he helped her. He gave her his cruiser boat. She already had a bunch of money from somewhere. They made it to St. Thomas.

She wanted to be away from civilization and people. This was not to Todd Rohrman's liking. He was a man who liked his carpeting, his cocktails at the lounge and a steady supply of fresh faces. But he was determined to stick with Dawn; she needed him. Sooner or later she would come to her senses and they'd move back to some city. Maybe Miami. And restart their careers.

Todd Rohrman never counted on Dawn's insanity and her viciousness, or on the unbreakable hold she had on him when he finally decided to get the hell away from her. Even when he wanted to leave, part of his mind made him stay. And organize her little New Age run-amuck cult.

Cults were so extreme and they required a lot of commitment. Todd was into a looser lifestyle, but he couldn't leave. He was still Dawn's personal assis-

tant. Somehow, he had become permanently en-
slaved to the role. He couldn't be content in the job,
even when Dawn the Priestess brought in the trappings of civilization, brought in construction work-
ers to build condominiums, brought in United States
citizens with money and taste. The whole thing was
foreign to Todd Rohrman. He played with the newcomers, but found they were too sincere for his
tastes. He liked his friends to be more…well, shallow.

He didn't feel good, either. Day after day he was
losing weight, and nothing he did seem to make him
feel better. It was like having the stomach flu for
twenty-two months.

But he did his job, didn't question the Priestess
too much, since she wasn't giving him answers any
longer. He didn't question the strange nature of the
village worship because he still saw it as nothing
more than a money-making stunt.

He didn't know or care why the worshipers came
and stayed. He didn't understand who the acolytes
were—just another necessary unpleasant aspect of
the whole unpleasant *thing*.

Todd Rohrman had somehow become the inter-
mediary between the Priestess and the people. Not
for her, the tending to daily maintenance tasks.
When the Priestess said that booze was forbidden,

Rohrman was the one who enforced it. Rohrman was the one who summoned the big new booze dealer to see the Priestess. He had hoped she would shake the man up, but she had been especially disoriented that morning. She had not understood why the man was even there. And now the booze dealer was returned to his condo without so much as a slap on the wrist.

Rohrman rocked slightly on his rope hammock and tried to settle his queasy stomach, but something told him he was not alone. He looked up, put his hand to his forehead to block the sun from his eyes, and found one of the acolytes.

"What do you want? I am trying to get some sun." He looked at his chest by way of explanation. His flesh had become very pale, living here in this jungle-swamp. He never seemed to get any pigment, no matter how much he lay out. Maybe this was a part of the sickness that seemed to plague him.

He felt as if he was withering.

The acolyte was staring at Rohrman.

Oh, that's all I need, Rohrman thought. One of these freaks getting randy for me. "Fine. Go away now."

The acolyte raised one hand across his own chest and pointed toward the village. Rohrman sighed and followed him to the entrance to the Priestess's private courtyards.

The acolyte materialized behind him without making a sound. Todd Rohrman wasn't impressed by these freaks. So what if they walked like Daniel Boone. "Business as usual. What is the problem?"

The acolyte pointed at the village and moved his hand to indicate all the villagers. They seem to be straying in one direction, away from the palace of the Priestess. Something was calling them to the far end of the settlement, and Rohrman knew what it was.

His day just kept getting worse.

He pounded on the door of the Priestess's private chamber. There was a faint sound from within and he entered. The Priestess looked up from her vanity. She spent hours there, every day. Not even putting on makeup!

She raised her eyebrows but said nothing.

"The liquor dealer is at it again, " Rohrman complained. "He's set up his bar in the forest. Are you going to do something about this guy or not?"

"What would I do and why?" the Priestess asked. She seemed lucid enough, but even in her clearest moments, these days, her mind was far away.

"Get rid of him. Send him packing. We don't need his kind here. You made the law, and you ought to enforce it."

The Priestess, the former Dawn Summens,

looked back into the antique mirror she had imported from France and brushed her beautiful hair. It was rich and dark with complex red highlights. Lustrous and shimmering. She still had the shell of the girl who did the seductive beach walk in the vacation commercials a few years ago. But that was all that was left now—the shell.

"I made this law?"

"Well, it wasn't me. But I do have a problem with rule-breakers. If you wanna change the rules, fine, but first let's teach this dude not to mess with authority."

"This is important to you."

Rohrman felt that the worst part of their relationship now was the formality of it all. Once, they had been able to say *anything* to each other. There had been almost no walls between them. Neither wanted anything from the other. He wasn't trying to get in her pants, and she had absolutely no interest in getting in his. It made for the ideal relationship. But that was all gone now.

"I guess it is," Rohrman said.

"Then handle it," she said, and looked back into her mirror.

Rohrman turned and almost collided with the acolyte. It was the tall one with the skin condition. "Why are you always getting in my damn way!

You freaks are more underfoot than a damn golden retriever!"

The acolyte bowed and backed away.

There was a steady stream of villagers returning from the forest with bags tucked under their arms. They seemed happy enough, and Todd had no real reason to want to keep the village dry. Hell, he drank every day. But then, he was in a different league from the worshipers.

But he had to punish the retailer for breaking Dawn's law. He would drive the guy out of town. That would make Joey Wild an example to the others. You could do almost anything you wanted in the village of the Priestess, and the lifestyle was pretty loose, but there were some rules. You had better follow those rules.

Todd Rohrman leaned a shoulder on the front of a condo and waited for the trickle of customers to subside.

Something that sounded like a heaving dog spoke from just over his shoulder. "What would you have us do?"

Leatherhead was still with him. The big freak was turning into Rohrman's little shadow. "What's it to you?"

"I would assist in enforcing the rules of the Priestess."

"Fine."

"We shall assassinate him."

Todd Rohrman laughed in spite of himself. "That's a little heavy-handed. I was thinking maybe we could just run his sorry ass out of town."

"Then he shall be driven away."

"But then I had a better idea," Rohrman continued. "Mr. Wild needs to really be made an example of to the other villagers. Don't you think?"

Leatherhead made no response. He simply laid his eyes on Rohrman and waited for further explanation.

"I think we need to hit him where it hurts most. In the retirement account. By the time he unloads his current inventory, he'll have a lot of cold cash needing to be deposited. I know for fact he has a runner take it back to the American bank in Ped for deposit.

"See, we waylay the runner in the swamp. Our friend Wild loses his profits. He comes out poorer than when he went into business today. You think one of you freaky boys can manage to relieve the courier of all his cash?"

"We shall relieve the courier of his cash," Leatherhead said.

"That will teach Mr. Wild a lesson, I guess."

Leatherhead didn't answer. The freak was already gone.

13

Tosh Cabby had his fifteen minutes of fame in the Olympics, running track. He did well, but he was never going to do that well again. The blood clot in his leg saw to that. He could still run track, and run far, even if he didn't have the speed he'd once had. There were still opportunities for a man with his talents. But many of the people he was closest to said he was wasting his life. They told him he wasn't rising to meet opportunities that were being handed to him.

Even his own mother wanted him to steal the money that was being entrusted to him on a daily basis. They didn't seem to understand, his mother, his uncles and cousins, every one, that he was in this career for the long haul. He could make a lot of money over a long period of time if he was patient and honest.

They said he was risking his life. They didn't

seem to understand that he was in no danger. No one who did business with the village of the Priestess was in danger. It was a fact of the jungle that the Priestess held sway. Those who went up against the Priestess suffered for it. There were rumors, and there was no lack of people claiming to have been victimized by the Priestess—or her protection spirits.

Tosh Cabby had witnessed firsthand what happened to those who tried to go against the Priestess. It wasn't the Priestess herself who was the danger. It was her acolytes. They were her enforcers. The freaks who clung to her side and did her bidding. They were vicious, savage men, and no one had any idea where they had come from.

Tosh Cabby had seen them and he was afraid of them—but he was glad they were around. Even though Tosh didn't dwell in the village, he did business with the village. That meant he was a part of the village—enough of a part that the Priestess's sphere of protection extended to him.

This gave him a high degree of security. He was safer transporting large amounts of cold cash through this part of Haiti than he would be taking business documents around the business district of Pedernales.

His family couldn't understand this. They couldn't understand how he managed to survive any single day when he was bringing money back from the Haitian village to the Dominican coastal town. Each time he left on such a mission, they expected him to not return.

And each time, they were amazed that he had failed to break open and investigate the contents of his pouch. The fact that he had taken it to the bank without even counting the amount of money he was handling, and deposit it into the bank box in middle of the night, was almost inexcusably foolish in their eyes. The amount of money in there might be enough to set him up for life—and enough to improve the lot of his poor, extended family.

"What kind of life would it set me up for?" Tosh Cabby asked them rhetorically.

Not for him the life of petty thievery. He didn't want to live in the United States. Even if he did take the money and use it to buy a new car or to put a down payment on a new house, what future did he have from there?

What the others didn't understand was that if he stayed here in this safe, protected role, he would prove himself to be a man of great trust. When the time came for the people of this foolish religion to move, they would remember him, and would remember his trustworthiness, and that would take Tosh Cabby to new and higher places.

But that kind of plan took patience.

And, after all, he was perfectly safe. No one outside the village would dare to touch someone protected by the village.

But what if the Priestess herself had some sort of problem with Tosh Cabby? It had never even occurred to him. Truth was, he should have thought of it a long time ago. But he had not. He had been a fool, after all—and he came to that revelation only at the moment he came upon one of the acolytes waiting for him in the mangrove swamp. The first indication that he was not alone was the sound of footsteps up in the trees. It wasn't an animal sound. It was a human sound, and it made him look up and down the narrow strip of dry earth that served as the swamp trail. Tosh saw the man in the trees, looking down at him. The strange man's knocking of knuckles on the tree trunk was a signal to some others.

At first, Tosh Cabby couldn't place the man. He was so odd in appearance. In a moment Tosh Cabby recalled that he had seen the man once, and once only, and it was standing in the village of the Priestess. Along with him had been the other acolytes.

Tosh Cabby was very afraid, and slightly confused. His mind insisted that he had no reason to be afraid, but his mind insisted, as well, that there was no reason that the Priestess's freaks should be following him through the swamps. It made no sense.

It seemed unlikely to be a coincidence, and yet it must be a coincidence. The freak just happened to be in a tree out in the swamps on a mission for the Priestess. After all, the swampy land left few dry stretches of ground for foot travel. There were only so many routes a traveler could take.

Treetop Man was chattering now, almost like a monkey, and almost as if he were calling to someone else. Tosh Cabby didn't know what to do. He simply kept running along, at a measured pace, hoping that he would leave the acolyte behind.

And that was what happened. The tree of Treetop Man fell away behind him, and minutes later he could no longer hear the chattering. He was alone again in the swamp. He breathed a sigh of relief, and put a new length into his stride. His legs were trained to run tirelessly for miles. He could travel these swamps faster than any other human on earth. Only the nagging prick of pain in his leg, which came from the place where the blood clot had healed over in his femoral artery, tended to slow him down sometimes. It had been enough to keep him out of the Olympics and other competitions, but not enough to interfere with his job today.

As fast as he was moving, no man should have

been able to catch up with him on foot. He heard no vehicle. And yet Treetop Man appeared again. Tosh heard the chattering high above his head. He saw Treetop Man bouncing up and down in the crux of a mangrove tree and looking back beyond Tosh Cabby, chattering with someone coming up behind.

Tosh Cabby was now terrified. Now he knew that there was something terribly wrong—and he understood that Treetop Man was not human. He was something else. All the acolyte freaks must be something more than human. The fact that Treetop Man was bouncing in the tree could only mean that he was bringing more of the acolytes to Tosh Cabby.

Tosh Cabby understood that the danger came from the village itself.

He ran faster. He took chances on leaf-strewed places in the trail where there could have been potholes in the trail to twist his ankle or muddy puddles that would suck his feet into the earth. He ate up more miles, then far above him was a commotion in the tree, and there was more swift movement and more chattering. Treetop Man was keeping pace in the mangrove treetops with the trained Olympian on the ground. How could he do that? Then Treetop Man came to the ground in the trail directly in front of Tosh.

Another one stepped out of the mangroves onto

the trail not ten paces behind him. It was the leader, who was seen many times wandering the village. Tosh knew they called him Leatherhead. He was an unsettling presence, but always silent and uninvolved in the hedonistic goings-on, so the villagers learned to ignore him.

Tosh addressed Leatherhead, since he was said to be the leader of the freaks. "What do you want? Have I done something to offend the Priestess?" he demanded.

He never got an answer. Leatherhead closed in on him with what could only be called menace, and Tosh Cabby knew he must defend himself at least. His only weapon was a hunting knife that he had found in the dump as a boy. It was coated with rust, but he kept the blade sharpened on stones. It was sharp enough to cut skin.

But there was a rumor about the one called Leatherhead, that his skin was tough and thick as tanned elephant hide and no blade would penetrate it. Now, the silly rumor sounded ominous. When Leatherhead took hold of him, Tosh sliced him in his bare abdomen. But nothing happened. There was just a fine white mark on the dark skin.

Leatherhead only held on to him until Treetop Man snatched him and up, up he went.

14

As soon as he had arranged for the delivery of the booze truck, Joey had also arranged for his regular courier to make a run to the village outskirts. You couldn't get reliably bonded couriers in the Dominican Republic, let alone Haiti, but the man he had worked with came highly recommended and had been reliable so far. He was a star athlete from the last track team that the Dominican Republic had sent to the Olympics. The guy came back with a silver medal and no prospects for the future. He now had a job running high-stakes packages around Hispaniola. It was said he never lost one. It was said he could get past bandits and border guards every time.

The setup was simple. Joey Wild had a bank account in the Dominican town of Pedernales. It was the local arm of a U.S. bank, and they had a night deposit box. The courier dropped them in. Once the funds were in his account, Joey got to see it on his telephone.

It was always a nervous period between the time his courier ran off into the mangroves and the time the deposit was reflected in his new bank balance.

The courier was just a kid, maybe nineteen, maybe twenty. A poor Dominican, put in a position of trust. Wild was handing over more cash than this kid had made in his life.

But what choice did Joey have? He couldn't keep this money with him. He couldn't stuff it into his mattress. Besides, as long as it was cold, hard cash, kept on his person, it wasn't real money. It was merely italics on the balance sheet in his head. It was not a true asset until it was in a bank, electronically tallied and secure.

"You'll get this into the deposit box tonight, right?"

"Yes sir," the kid said. "I always do."

"I know. Okay." Joey Wild knew that he shouldn't belabor the point, or the kid might wonder exactly what he was worried about. He might realize he was carrying quite lot of money and be tempted to break the seal on the pouch and count the cash inside. When he counted it, it might be enough to convince the kid that now was the time to make that break he'd been planning on. The money he had in the pouch would get him to the United States, buy him a car, even give him a down payment on a house. It was a lot of cash.

But the kid was a good kid. He had never let Joey down before and he'd done maybe five courier jobs for him already. He could trust the kid.

But it was gonna be a long night.

It sure was a long night. Joey Wild must have checked his bank records a dozen times between dusk and dawn, even though common sense told him that there was no way the money was going to hit his account overnight. He had to wait until the morning, when the bank opened the box, when the tellers made their way through the night deposits.

Eight o'clock, Joey Wild dialed the bank. The bank would be opening now. His account didn't show the deposit yet. No reason it should, he told himself.

Eight-thirty. No change on the balance in his account. He wasn't worried about it yet. The tellers never worked that fast. His previous night deposits were never posted before nine.

Nine o'clock. No change on the balance. No record of the deposit. Joey Wild began to sweat.

Nine-fifteen. His deposit didn't show up. Nine-thirty. The balance remained the same.

Joey Wild called the bank.

"I am sorry, sir," the bank manager said, being polite, knowing he was talking to one of his best customers. "They are working on the night box now."

"How many night deposits can there be? It's the Dominican Republic!" Joey Wild snapped.

"You would be surprised, sir," the bank manager said, refusing to be insulted. "There are several deposits remaining to be processed."

"Can you at least check for me, pal?"

"No, sir. It is bank policy for the teller and the teller manager to handle night deposit without interruption. It is a matter of security."

At ten o'clock, Wild's balance was unchanged. He redialed.

"You better not try to tell me that night box is still not done."

"All deposits are processed and entered. Your deposit was not in the night deposit box."

"Bullshit!"

"I'll check myself," the bank manager said. Joey Wild waited on hold and paced back and forth in his little condo, feeling claustrophobic in the tiny space for the first time since moving in. His studio was no bigger than the master bathroom suite in the house his wife had kicked him out of.

He needed to go outside, in the open, walk around, but he couldn't let people see him like this. He couldn't let on that he had lost his money—especially after getting the blessing of the Priestess to continue his business.

The bank manager was back. "Sir, every deposit has been processed, and there are no discrepancies. There are no missing pouches. There is no deposit slip from you, sir. I believe your courier may have been delayed."

Joey Wild snapped shut the phone. His courier had not been delayed. His courier had absconded with Wild's money.

15

The pain that Tosh Cabby suffered seemed to have no end. He wasn't bleeding, so he couldn't bleed to death. He could only tremble with agony. He felt his feet bound together and he felt the world was upside down. He was hanging in the trees, swaying gently. He didn't have the strength to lift his dangling arms to touch the places where he felt broken. His feet had gone from painful to ice-cold during his first hour of hanging, and now he couldn't feel them at all.

He knew there was a familiar aching in his legs where his body liked to make blood clots. It was making one for him now as a result of the injury.

He should have been taking his blood thinners, but the danger of being wounded in the swamps and bleeding to death was too great. Besides, why should he worry about blood clots when he was as active as he was? He had never counted on having his legs bound in a tourniquet.

The clots would get bigger and float into his bloodstream eventually, looking for a place to lodge.

Tosh hoped a clot would lodge in his heart. His heart would become blocked and quickly go into arrest. It would be a miserable death, but it would at least be quicker than the long-suffering agony if the clot lodged in his lung and he suffocated slowly, or the lingering madness of a stroke if it lodged in his brain.

He whiled away the miserable hours recalling his anatomy lessons in school. Once he had been taught how the blood flowed through the body. Depending on where the clot was, it might be on a direct path into his brain. That would not be a good thing. If it were forced into his brain and formed a blockage, what part of his brain would it block? What brain function would he lose? His memories? His speech? His bodily functions?

He remembered a next-door neighbor who'd had a stroke. She was fine one day and a near vegetable the next. She forgot how to talk, and her left side seemed to have forgotten how to work at all. Her legs would go out from under her, and her left arm hung limp and lifeless. When the doctor came, days later, he had asked her stupid questions. "Tell me your name," he'd demanded. "Tell me the kinds of the animals in your yard. How many fingers am I holding up?"

The poor woman had been unable to make a single coherent sound, let alone speak the word "Mildred" or "chicken."

But all through the night, as the swelling thing in his leg seemed to grow, Tosh Cabby talked to himself. He named animals. He said the alphabet. His words sounded fine to him. Then it occurred to him that maybe, if he started having a stroke, and his words became jumbled, he might not even be able to tell that they were not the right words.

At dawn he fell into unconsciousness.

"Wake up."

Someone was slapping his face. Tosh Cabby's eyes fluttered, but his head was swollen with so much blood they would barely open.

"Where's my money?" Joey Wild demanded.

Tosh Cabby croaked, "Goat."

"What?" Wild demanded.

"Goat," Tosh Cabby repeated.

Wild sneered. "Goat? What does that mean?"

Cabby felt a wave of relief. He could still talk! The clot had not lodged in his brain. And his heart still beat and his lungs seemed to be functioning.

But his physical agony came back to him. His legs screamed from the pain, and he realized that he could no longer feel his feet or shins below the place where they were wrapped in stiff rope that dangled him from a high tree branch. Treetop Man had strung him up high enough to put him almost out of Joey Wild's reach.

"Help me down."

"Answer the question," Wild said. "Where's my money?"

"They took it."

"Who?"

"The Priestess's freaks. Leatherhead and Tree-top Man."

"No way," Wild said. "Me and the Priestess, we got an agreement."

"Why would I lie?"

The kid had a point about that, Wild admitted. The courier was in bad shape. There wasn't much of a chance this was some sort of a staged diversion the courier had set up to deflect guilt from himself for taking the money. Wild was steaming mad as he turned back to the village.

"Hey!" the courier croaked.

Joey Wild stomped back to the kid. "Guess I gotta take care of your sorry ass," Wild complained.

"I have clotty blood. I form clots when I get injured. I must get to a hospital."

"Now, how am I supposed to accomplish that? Tell you what—I'll get you down from there and you get yourself to the hospital." Wild clambered up the steplike roots and branches of the mangrove and tugged on the dangling loop of rope. The knot melted. The courier plummeted headfirst to the ground, and would have cracked open his skull if the knot hadn't tightened again and brought him to a jarring stop a few inches from the earth. Wild picked the knot again until it slipped open and the courier collapsed on the trail.

"Don't leave me," the courier called as Wild stomped away.

Wild came back, saying, "*Now* what?"

"I need a hospital."

"So come to the village and you can bum a ride to the hospital."

"My legs are dead."

Wild examined the black, swollen bags of flesh that were squeezing out of the straining running shoes. "Blood flow cut off by the rope," Wild pointed out. "Need to get that blood flowing again."

"No, don't do it!" The courier weakly tried batting Wild's hands away from the ropes binding his knees. "The blood in my legs is dead and poison. Don't let it into my body."

"You got to get the circulation back in those feet if you ever want to walk again," Wild insisted, and he slipped the knot and pulled off the rope.

Maybe, he decided, the kid was right. The feet did

not look alive. But how could they be dead just from hanging in a tree for a while?

The courier laid his head back and made ungodly sounds as the rotting blood from the decaying flesh of his feet oozed into his bloodstream. Wild gave him a minute, clutching doggedly to the notion that everything would be all right again once the circulation was restored.

"They're not, dead, I swear to you. Just really, really asleep," Wild promised.

The courier wasn't listening.

The truth was, Joey Wild was eager to get back to the village and find his cash pouch—and find out why, exactly, the Priestess had violated their agreement. "You know, just the other night I slept on my arm the wrong way. I get up to go to the john and my arm is flopping around at my side and I can't make it move and I said to myself, 'This is really gonna hurt,' and you better believe it did. The blood started going back into it and it tingled like I never felt it tingle. So I know exactly what you're going through."

The courier was bleeding from the mouth. He had bitten into his tongue.

"I'll admit, you probably have a worse case. But you just give it a few more minutes, let the circulation get back to normal, and you'll be on your feet again. Ten minutes, you'll be good as new."

The courier had a swelling black knot on his neck, too. That didn't look healthy. It seemed to be swelling with every passing second. Wild didn't have time to deal with this.

"So, I'm sure you'll be right behind me. I'll run on ahead and find the doc, and he'll be waiting for you when you get there. Get you all fixed up again."

The courier opened his eyes wide, the brown pupils hidden by bloody veins, and gaped at the morning sky.

"See ya," Wild said, and sprinted away before the whole situation became even more awkward.

16

Remo stopped about a mile into the mangrove preserve. He had been waved through by the U.S. military post, who seemed confused by his lack of cargo. When he tried to explain that he wasn't a drinking man, they were only more confused.

He got out of the SUV alongside the rutted trail that he was assured was the road to the village of the Priestess of the Dawn, although it was unmarked. He got down on his knees and bent low over the front tire, picking at the treads with his fingernails.

There was nothing wrong with the tire; his eyes were actually examining the skyline of mangrove trees. There was a man in a tree about a hundred yards away, dressed in simple brown britches and shirt that seemed to match his skin, and the man was watching Remo. He moved through the trees like a monkey, on all fours, and came to a higher perch to view Remo better.

Finally, Remo stood and stared directly at the man, who became alarmed when he saw he had been spotted. He scampered into the branches like a spider and vanished.

Remo got under way again, thinking about the ugly man in the tree. The little man had moved extraordinarily fast, faster than almost anyone should have been able to move.

The presence of a strange little man in the trees was a bigger problem than Remo wanted to consider. He wanted to leave this place, get back home and check on Chiun. He couldn't stand thinking that Chiun was back home, sick, and he was out here doing busywork.

He had known Chiun for years. There was no one he cared about more on this earth. Remo had known Chiun since being recruited by CURE. Decades ago, when Remo Williams came back from his tour of duty and became a cop, his life seemed on track until he was framed for murder. His trial was rammed through the legal system with unprecedented speed, and he popped out the other end to land in death row. Other inmates languished on death row for years, their fate stalled by legal appeals and protracted legal machinations. It wasn't like that for Remo Williams. Before he knew it, he was being prepped for execution.

Remo didn't understand exactly what had happened him. He only knew he'd been framed for a murder he didn't commit. His fiancée and his friends were gone, and he'd never had a family. There was no support on hand, and the machinery of justice was running at full speed. Remo was resigned to being murdered for a murder he wasn't guilty of.

Then a priest came to offer him comfort on his last day on earth, and told Remo that death could be overcome. All it took was a little pill. This wasn't the same message of resurrection Remo knew so well from the nuns who'd raised him.

Remo took the pill from the priest and, as directed, held it in his mouth as he was strapped into the electric chair. He bit down on it when the electricity was shot through his body. Remo didn't remember exactly what happened after that.

What happened was that Remo was declared dead and his body was carted away. As far as the State of New Jersey was concerned, Remo Williams was a successfully executed killer.

Remo wasn't as dead as they thought, and he woke up in prison in the training facilities at Folcroft Sanitarium, in Rye, New York. The priest who'd provided him with the pill turned out to be a CIA agent by the name of Conrad MacCleary. He gave Remo Williams the option of joining a federal agency named CURE as an undercover assassin or of being assassinated himself. Remo really didn't have much of a choice. He took the job, and he began to train as the enforcement arm on the smallest and most secret federal intelligence agency ever.

His training included weapons and espionage techniques. His most important training came from a small, impossibly old Korean man who was some sort of martial-arts expert. He had the fastest-ever reflexes Remo had ever seen, and he moved like no other human being on earth could move.

Remo didn't like this Chiun at first. Chiun had a superior, smug attitude and he was nearly always insulting. But his skills were incredible and he taught Remo well. At some point, Chiun persuaded the director of CURE to dismiss the other instructors and give him complete responsibility for Remo's training. Chiun said his was the only training Remo required.

Chiun was correct.

Remo didn't understand at the time why Chiun had such a compelling interest in his training. He took it as a matter of course. It was years before he found out the entire truth.

Chiun wasn't in that the habit of renting himself out as a trainer of commandos. Only to satisfy the truth of an old Sinanju prophecy did Chiun find it necessary to reveal his secrets to a young, meat-eating, uncivilized Caucasian adult.

It was said in the legend of the village of Sinanju that one day there would appear a Master who didn't come from the village. For the first time in all history, this Master would be a White man, not a Korean. He would come from across the sea—naturally, as this was where all white men came from. And he would be the greatest of all the Sinanju Masters.

Chiun came reluctantly to America, and it was not just the prophecy that compelled him. It was an act of desperation. Master Chiun, already quite old, had already lost two possible successors. First his own son, just barely entering his training to be a Master, had died.

Chiun had recruited another member of his family. As always, it was a male youth, as tradition demanded. The boy was trained for years, to adulthood, to the level of Master, only to betray Chiun and the tradition of Sinanju and abandon his people. Chiun was left old, with no successor, and in shame. He risked leaving this world with no Master to succeed him. Chiun risked severing the ancient lineage.

But the rumors of the skills of the Sinanju Masters had reached the ears of a drunkard spy, Conrad

MacCleary, who contacted Chiun in the village of Sinanju in North Korea, and requested that he come to America to train a newly recruited assassin in the ways of Sinanju. Chiun shouldn't have accepted the offer, but he did.

He would come to America, and he would see if there was any way that this so-called assassin could possibly be the prophesized white Master of Sinanju.

Remo Williams was an unpromising specimen at first, but he learned his early lessons quickly. This was a small miracle in itself. He learned despite being an adult and despite being unfamiliar with the philosophies of Sinanju, which were drilled at an early age into the heads of potential trainees.

But Remo, the large-headed American, continued to learn the art from Chiun. He continued to excel, and he was eventually trained to the point of excellence in his skills. He earned the right to be called a Master of Sinanju. And finally, after years with the Master's rank, Chiun surrendered to him the title of ultimate authority; Remo Williams became Reigning Master of Sinanju.

They had endured much together, Chiun and Remo, throughout their years together. Now they continued to function as the enforcement arm of CURE, but to Remo his role was changed. Now he was heir to the legacy of Sinanju. He felt loyalty to his country, but he didn't feel as if he had a lifelong dedication to CURE. He had responsibilities elsewhere. Not even just in the village of Sinanju, for the old legend had expanded since the time he had first learned of it.

Now, there was a second village, this one on a Native American reservation in Arizona, founded centuries before by a self-exiled Master of Sinanju who came to America before Columbus. This ancient Master had established his own tradition among the people he joined. His legacy continued to this day, in a peace-loving people with extraordinary skills. The head of the clan was a man known as Sunny Joe Roam. Once upon a time, he had been a Hollywood stunt man. He was also Remo Williams's biological father, as Remo and Chiun finally learned.

Sunny Joe lived to this day on the reservation, where he shared his home with Remo's adult children, the young man Winston, and the young woman named Freya.

But Chiun remained the most important figure in Remo's life. Chiun had become a father to him, and a mentor and role model. And now, Chiun was ill. Chiun was quite likely dying. And Chiun was denying it all.

Remo had no proof of this, of course. No doctor

had examined Chiun and pronounced him sick with some disease. But Chiun and Remo had run into a situation that had convinced Remo that there was an illness lingering inside Chiun's body. Perhaps the cancer or whatever it was had not even begun to reproduce or damage the ancient Master's body yet, but it was there, waiting to be activated. Chiun claimed it was another of Remo's uninformed assumptions—just one of the many wrong conclusions Remo was prone to.

But why shouldn't Chiun be sick? The man probably held some sort of record as being the oldest human being on the planet. He was healthier than most men were at age twenty, but even Masters of Sinanju couldn't last forever. And Chiun was already pushing the envelope, even by Sinanju longevity standards.

Remo felt sick himself, thinking of Master Chiun wasting away from some disease. He wanted to do something about it. He wanted to be looking for answers. He didn't want to be driving around a swamp in Haiti visiting monkey men and hippies.

He was certain that the name of the cult was a coincidence. It had to be. How could it *not* be? So, he had convinced himself that coming to the village was pointless. He'd get in, snoop around and report to Smith that this was all a waste of time. Which it had to be.

But then he thought about the man in the tree.

What was the deal with that? Was it just some quick-moving Haitian kid? Was there some back-woods community that spent their lives in the mangrove trees, learning to climb like the monkeys?

That had to be it.

Remo saw another one of them. It was nestled in another mangrove a mile ahead and staring at Remo.

Remo braked and stuck his head out the window. He could see the man perfectly. It was the same man.

Nobody could move as fast as an SUV in a mangrove swamp. No regular human being anyway. Not even frickin' Tarzan could cover the ground that fast.

But it was most definitely the same individual Monkey Man that Remo had seen several miles back.

Remo wished his eyesight were not so good. He wished that he could convince himself he was mistaken about the identity of the Monkey Man. But he couldn't ignore the fact. His eyesight was better than that of any human on earth. He could see the man perfectly, even in a tree a mile way, and see that it was the same man, with the same lines on his face, the exact same bone structure.

Once again, Remo was less mystified by the nature of the little man than he was annoyed by the fact that this meant he was going to have to linger awhile and figure out the mystery.

When he reached the village of the Priestess, Remo Williams was in a foul mood.

17

Joey Wild felt a little guilty about leaving the courier in the forest, and his own guilt made him feel even more angry. He wasn't pissed off enough to not feel afraid as he stomped into the village and headed for the Priestess's mansion. He arrived at the stone entrance just in time to see the procession of freaks marching into the courtyard.

There was a new freak at the head of the procession. Joey had never seen this one before. He was a lot more normal-looking than the other freaks. In fact, he was completely normal except for the immense wrists. Maybe he was into some new kind of physical conditioning that Joey had never heard of.

Not that he cared.

As he entered the outer courtyard uninvited, the freaks were going into the inner courtyard and closing the door behind them. Before Joey could decide what to do, Todd Rohrman entered from an unnoticed side door with his folding chair.

Wild knew him as the pansy-ass, unfriendly assistant of the Priestess, and he was the guy who seemed to have it in for Wild's distribution business.

"Hey."

Rohrman spared him a glance and looked at the sky, then maneuvered his folding chair a few inches to the right.

"I'm talking to you."

"I wish you wouldn't."

"You stole my money."

"I don't think so. You're stealing my sun time. You know I get about an hour a day of good sun? It's because of all the mother-effing mangroves. I missed my chance yesterday, but I'll be damned if I'll miss this one. So you go away now."

"I want my money."

"I don't have your money."

"Liar."

REMO COULD HEAR the argument outside, but was more interested in the Priestess, who now entered the wide chamber just inside the mansion's double doors. Maybe it had been a receiving hall a hundred years ago. Today it was filled with the accoutrements of a very confused young woman.

She moved like a sleepwalker until her eyes fell on Remo. Then she crossed to him and stood before him, peering into his face.

"It is you," she said. "Hello, Remo."

"Hello, you," Remo said. He recognized her, but the name wouldn't seem to come back to him now. He tried to picture her—where had he seen her last? For some reason, he kept seeing her in a bikini on a beach. It was a nice recollection. Then he recalled eating lunch with her. Where? When?

"Union Island, right?" he said with a finger snap. "You had noodles. I had rice."

Now Remo remembered Dawn Summens quite well. She was fun to look at, for all the right reasons. She had a lithe figure without being scrawny. Her skin had the gloss of some kind of rich, highly polished wood, but then there were those freckles. Almost too many of them. She was unique and arresting. Her hair was rich and dark, with little glints of red, perfectly complementing the luster of her skin. Her eyes were blue-green, the color of the turquoise Caribbean Sea.

The minister of tourism and professional bikini model looked too good to be true, and if you happened to catch one of her television commercials for Union Island vacations you would automatically assume she was not true. Those eyes had to be contact lenses. That skin had to be computer-colored. Those boobs must be man-made.

And her dialogue on those commercials. She would make this come-hither little smile and say, "I am Union Island. Come to me."

A guy got itches in his britches just hearing her say that. Remo wasn't exactly Joe Six-Pack, but he was still a red-blooded, mostly American male, and Dawn Summens's commercials did the same thing to him they did to most other guys, and who cared if she had contact lenses and breast implants?

But when you met her, she was genuine. The suntan was real, the eyes were unaltered and the boobs swayed in a way that proved there was no kind of artificial support system installed under the skin.

Remo had met Dawn Summens under the most ideal conditions possible, on one of the better stretches of Union Island beach. The bikini model was wearing, of all things, a bikini. Even better than on the commercials, she was wearing only the bottom piece.

Remo Williams had treated Dawn Summens to lunch—she donned the bikini top first—and he never, ever touched her. He never even found out for sure if she was part of Greg Grom's scheme to turn Union Island into an independent nation and personal cash cow.

"You do remember me?"

"Sure. Sorry I never called—somebody told me you died."

"You did not come to my funeral."

"Well, you know, it wasn't like we had even known each other all that long. We just had lunch that one day. And then there were all the problems. People dying—lots of them. Not just you, you know. It gave me the willies. I got off that island."

"They buried me in it," the Priestess said.

"You don't say." Remo wanted her to keep talking. He was trying to figure her out. Her eyes and pulse were rampant and irregular. It was as if she was on drugs, although he couldn't smell anything.

"When I woke up, I was in a coffin in the ground. I was buried alive. And I had to fight my way out."

"But you made it," Remo said. "I have to hand it to you. That took spunk. Most people would have just said to hell with it and died. How did you manage it? I mean, what did you breathe all that time?"

Dawn Summens became agitated. Remo could sense it. Her heart pounded and her breathing became rapid and her eyes flickered in their sockets. "I found a cavity in the adjoining crypt. The coffins had rotted away and opened up in the earth, and there was enough air to breathe. Barely. I almost died anyway. It was a disturbing experience."

"Being dead is disturbing in general," Remo said. "Ask me how I know."

"When I was out of the earth and under the night sky, and I realized that I had done it and had lived through it all, something came to me. It was sort of a revelation. It was akin to being suddenly filled with a new consciousness. It was almost like being possessed by some wonderful spirit. And something came to me in that moment," Dawn Summens said. "Out of nowhere. It was a name. Remo. It is a name I have exalted and proclaimed around the world."

"Yes, I wanted to ask you about that," Remo said. "It seemed a little odd to me, for somebody to name a religion Remo. It doesn't make sense. I can count on one hand the number of Remos I've met in my life. I was hoping you could explain it."

"It simply came to me. It was the right thing to do."

Remo was still not quite sure what the deal was. It still didn't make sense to him—and it was only the first point of discussion on his list. There was also the fact of the dark-skin freakazoids. Remo was pretty sure they hadn't been hanging around with Dawn Summens the last time they met.

The argument outside changed tenor. Remo gathered that one man had accused the other man of stealing his money. It had something to do with broken rules. The man whose money was stolen was angry. He seemed to think the other man was someone in charge and someone with an inside track to the Priestess.

Dawn's assistant kept talking about wanting to get his suntan.

Then the argument became physical. Remo heard the sounds of one man handling another by his clothing, and shaking him violently. It was Dawn's assistant who was getting manhandled, and his snootiness turned to pleading. Now the voices reached inside the Priestess's home.

The Priestess turned to her circle of freaks, one after another.

Her eyes rested finally on the small, brown mouse of a man. He was a strange one, Remo thought, but only as strange as the others. He couldn't figure out their metabolism, either. They were just as strange in a way that was different from the way Dawn Summens was strange.

This one acted as if he was intoxicated, although there was no smell of alcohol in the air. He was wavering on his feet, his eyes bloodshot, and he had a hard time keeping his vision focused. When the Priestess nodded at him, the little mouse of a man collapsed on the floor as lifeless as a sack of sticks.

No one moved. The Priestess—Dawn Summens,

Remo reminded himself—did not seem alarmed. Apparently the collapse was not unusual. In fact, there seemed to be little difference in the physiology of the collapsed man. His heartbeat and breathing remained constant. Just as baffling was his motionlessness.

Remo knew that most human beings had a difficult time relaxing their bodies. When they crawled into bed to sleep, their bodies were tense. Even in sleep, human beings flexed their muscles and tensed their bodies, and even moved their limbs sometimes to replicate the action in their dreams. It was virtually impossible for a human being to be completely relaxed, especially instantly. And yet the man on the floor was absolutely motionless. No muscles were flexed.

Almost instantly, the voice of Dawn's assistant changed from whining to belligerent. It was the same voice box, but it sounded as if it was being operated by a different human being.

"What is it you want?" the assistant demanded.

His attacker explained again how his money had been stolen from the courier in the jungle. He accused the Priestess's freaks of stealing the money. "We had an agreement, the Priestess and me."

"What sort of agreement?"

"You go ask the Priestess. Then you come back and give me my money."

"Wait one moment," the assistant said.

Dawn's assistant went through another personality shift. "For the love of God, don't hurt me."

"I'll wring your fucking neck unless I get my money back right now."

"I don't have your money. I don't even know what you're talking about."

The attacker was enraged now. "How many times do I have to explain it to you?"

The collapsed man on the floor rose to his feet, without changing his respiration or pulse. He stepped close to the Priestess, and the tallest freak with the really bad complexion stepped in to join the huddle. In hushed voices, the mousy man explained the altercation in the courtyard.

The voices in the huddle were too low to be heard by normal ears, but Reno Williams heard them. He knew what it meant, even if he didn't understand how it had happened. The little man had gone into the body of Dawn's assistant, had ascertained the nature of the argument and had come back to report.

But how?

Another damn mystery. There was something really strange going on here. He knew he had to figure it all out.

The tall one with the bad skin left the room,

passed through a pair of doors and Remo overheard
the conversation change in the courtyard.

"You?" the attackers said. "I am not talking to
you. I'm going to talk to the Priestess and nobody
else."

There was no response from the freak. Dawn's assistant gagged. "He's choking me."

Remo heard the scrape of metal on leather, and
pictured the dagger that hung on the belt of the man
with the bad skin.

"Back off, or I break his neck. I said, back off."

Dawn's assistant pleaded, "Please back off!"

But the last word was cut off. There was a pop—
a bone pop that Remo knew well. He guessed that
the man with the bad skin had not backed off. Then
Remo heard the rapid footsteps of the attacker flee-
ing from the yard.

Through it all, Remo kept his face still. As far as
Dawn Summens or her freaky friends knew, he was
totally oblivious to what was happening outside.

The man with the bad skin returned and whispered to the Priestess. He was reporting the flight of
the one named Wild. Wild had slain the one called
Rohrman.

Rohrman, Remo knew for a fact, was still alive
and gasping for breath on the ground in front of the
Priestess's house. Not that there was much that

could be done for him at this point, what with his snapped spine, but it was interesting to watch how the group responded to the news.

Dawn waved her fingers at one of the other freaks. More whispers. Dawn told this one to keep watch on the one named Wild. The freak bowed his head and left, but Remo saw enough of his face to recognize it. It was the monkey man he had seen in the trees. Monkey Man left the room, and outside Remo heard an abrupt, strange sound. It was like someone jumping from the earth, but there was no sound of that someone landing on the earth again. There was only the fall of footsteps in the mangroves overhead.

18

Joey Wild fought his own addiction as he ran for his life. He was addicted to the village, and he didn't understand where it had come from. He hadn't realized the addiction even existed until this moment. Even as he faced death, his urge to flee to safety was almost overcome by his urge to return to the village.

He'd understood it a little earlier today when he had left village and battled the almost physical compulsion to stay behind. The only thing that had enabled him to overcome the urge was the knowledge that he would be returning shortly. Go into the preserve, look for the courier, come back.

This time he was running away from the village with the assurance that he could never return. His anger had undone his future there.

His anger was a strange thing in itself. Wild was no killer. And yet his anger had been such that he had twisted the neck of that man without mercy.

And now the Priestess's freaks would surely do the same to him unless he got far away from the village before they caught up. Joey Wild didn't think they would be able to catch him. They seemed like a slow-moving bunch of freaks. The courier had been nabbed using trickery, he was sure. But they wouldn't get Wild that way. They were back there. He knew it for a fact. He was up here. All he had to do was run, run, run.

But he didn't want to run—he wanted to stay—and he found himself on a trail he had never meant to take. It headed back in the direction of the village. He forced himself to turn away.

It *was* an addiction. He was addicted to the village. He didn't understand it, and he didn't have time to figure it out now. He was terrified that his subconscious would overcome his common sense, and he would return to the village and certain death.

He tried to think of what was ahead of him. After many miles he would leave the old-growth section of the preserve and enter the sparser new growth. There he would find a Jeep trail. He could jog along it. Or walk—it was another five miles to the checkpoint at the edge of the preserve. There would be U.S. military there. Thank God. They'd protect him.

Joey Wild was startled to hear a ruckus in the trees above him. When he looked up, nothing was there. He kept running, and when he heard the something in the trees again, something big, he knew he was in danger.

Soon enough he spotted the acolyte. The man was standing in a tree ahead of him. It was the one called Treetop Man, of course. Joey had never thought much about the freak's nickname, but it was clear to him now.

Treetop Man craned his neck then, up out of the tree, and disappeared into the mass of leaves overhead. There was stillness. And then the trees opened up and Treetop Man looked down at Joey Wild from a new perch and grinned.

Joey Wild ran, and the branches rattled on either side of him. He pictured Treetop Man swinging himself through the jungle like a monkey or flinging himself from branch to branch like a flying squirrel.

However he moved, his speed was so great that he made rings around Joey Wild.

Then something came out of the trees and flopped on the ground at Joey's feet. He snatched it up. It was his money pouch. Unopened. He could feel the stacks of bills inside.

Joey Wild could see two reasons that they had returned the cash. One was giving him back what was rightfully his as a sort of gesture of restitution. The second was to taunt him before they enacted their punishment.

Joey Wild didn't believe for an instant that he was being given restitution.

Treetop Man was right above him. Joey Wild flung the cash pouch down. "Take it. I don't want it anymore."

Treetop Man simply reached down and took him by the wrist and Joey was lifted off the trail. A rope was noosed on his ankle. It was the same hard hemp rope that had been used on the courier.

Treetop Man had the other end of the rope in one hand, and when Treetop Man jumped up, up, out of sight with amazing speed, the rope went with him. The noose tightened on Joey's ankle and pulled it skyward with such force that Joey Wild's leg popped right off of his body.

19

Dawn Summens's galloping heart rate flagged and she slumped, her bottom landing on a vanity stool. It was as if her energy had just run out.

Remo felt all eyes upon him. It was as if Dawn Summens and her freaky friends were waiting for him to make the next move.

"Well, here I am. Now what?"

"I want nothing of you, Remo."

"Listen, sweetheart, you've got to have some reason for starting this Holy Mother of the Dawn business and some reason for naming it Remo, of all things. It must have something to do with me, right? It doesn't seem like a coincidence."

"But I told you it was not. I explained how the name came to me. There is a meaning to it, Remo, but I do not know what the meaning is."

"Okay," Remo said. "Just answer me this. What's the reason for *any* of it?"

Dawn Summens seemed to lose some of her clarity. "I worship the goddess. I worship all the gods. I'll welcome all those who wish to come and join me. I provide for them if they wish to stay, so that they will be unencumbered by the mechanisms of life that could drag them away. I ask of them that they worship the goddess and the gods with me."

"What goddess? What gods?"

"The Goddess of the Dawn," Dawn Summens said, but she was fading away from Remo. Her mind was drifting off.

"Hey! Pay attention! I'm getting a little irritated here!" Remo said. "You name a religion after me, for some reason, then you go and worship yourself. But you don't have the good sense to explain why. What are *you* supposed to get out of all this?"

"I want nothing. I simply wish to worship the goddess in the company of my acolytes and any others who choose to come here."

"You said that."

"Worship her in my own way."

"So why'd you drag me into it!"

"I don't know."

"I am not buying that, sweetheart," Remo said. "In fact, I don't think you are buying it yourself."

"I am only the Priestess. I do not have all the answers. I do not have complete understanding. I only know my own convictions, Remo."

"You're a nut job," Remo snapped.

"Yes," Dawn Summens murmured, and an invisible speck of dust seemed to take her attention as it crossed the room. "When will we reach capacity in the village?" she asked no one in particular.

"Three days," the one with the bad skin said.

"Remo. You will stay with us three days," Dawn Summens said. "I will sleep now."

"Already? I thought we could talk. Catch up on old times."

"I sleep first." In fact, she was almost falling asleep where she sat.

The freak with the bad skin showed Remo Williams the door.

THE FREAK with the bad skin didn't even have the courtesy to offer Remo a guided tour of the retreat. Remo took a stroll, trying not to let his agitation overcome him. He didn't want to be here. He wanted to go home and be with Chiun. He didn't really care about monkey men or freaks with bad skin. He didn't even care about Dawn Summens. She was obviously missing a few marbles, and there was obviously something here that wasn't right—but none of it mattered when faced with the tragedy that waited at home.

Chiun was sick, but he denied it up and down. And Chiun wasn't exactly showing signs of distress. The old man was as active as ever. And active, for a Master of Sinanju Emeritus, was as fit as any Olympian athlete on earth.

That was part of the problem. Chiun was so strong and fit that it was impossible to see if he was developing any weaknesses. Remo watched the old Master closely, ever sensitive to the first indication of any serious illness. Chiun sensed Remo's watching and was insulted, of course. Chiun maintained up and down that he wasn't sick, only that Remo's pestering was making him that way.

So there wasn't a thing that Remo could do about it, except keep close to the old man and watch for the inevitable sign.

But he had thought it might do him good to get his mind off of the problem by coming out to Haiti. It wasn't doing him good. It was eating him up. And now he was obligated to hang around and find out what was behind the freak show and why, oh, why, it was named after *him*, of all people.

The sooner he figured it out then the sooner he could head back to Piney Point, and Master Chiun.

Right now he had a hint. He would track down the man who had caused all the fuss in the yard and broken the neck of Dawn's assistant.

Remo wandered about the village, apparently just curious, but he could sense he was being followed. It was one of the freaks, of course. Remo came to a long, low pavilion with a pagoda-like roof and walls of mosquito screens. Inside, on mounds of cushions, a well-attended orgy was going on. Remo tried to count the bodies and gave up at thirty. What surprised him was the man-to-woman ratio. It was nearly one to one, and most of them weren't bad to look at. Some were stunning.

How was Dawn Summens persuading attractive women to live the sleazy lifestyle? And what was the point of the whole cult, anyway?

He pretended to be very interested and made his way slowly around the perimeter of the pavilion. He soon had the attention of half the women inside. They flocked to the mosquito netting, urging him to come inside. Remo backed off as he put the pavilion between himself and the freak who was tailing him, and then he slipped into the mangroves.

Remo Williams moved like a jungle cat, slipping around among the underbrush and making no disturbance that could ever be followed. He circled the village until he was outside the nineteenth-century stone building that was Dawn Summens's private home, then penetrated the jungle in the direction of a certain smell. The smell was also attracting many flies.

A few miles outside the village, Remo found the corpse tucked high up in a mangrove.

"HIYA, SMITTY," Remo said. "You'll never guess where I'm calling from."

Smith said, "The mangrove preserve. Approximately 4.3 miles northwest of the village. Have you entered the village yet, Remo?"

"I mean, guess where I'm *really* calling from. A tree. I'm up in a tree. I'm not by myself. My friend here is from the village. I'm borrowing his phone."

"His name is Joseph Emeril Wild, according to the registration on the cell phone you are calling from. Is he listening to our conversation?" Smith asked testily.

"Maybe his ghost is. He was recently snuffed by the Priestess's bodyguards. They are a strange lot, Smitty. Very strange. But wait until you find out about the Priestess. Somebody we know. You'll never guess that, either."

After a pregnant pause, Smith said, "I do not wish to guess."

"Dawn Summens. Remember her? She was the bikini model in the commercials for Union Island. She was minister of tourism, too. We never did quite figure out if she was in on the whole scheme with Greg Grom to shaft the United States."

If Smith was surprised by the revelation, he didn't show it. "Go on."

"She was dead," Remo said. "That's what she claims, anyway. She says she dug herself out of the grave. We heard she was dead, too—remember, Smitty?"

Remo could hear Smith snapping out commands on his keyboard. "I do recall, Remo. Ms. Summens was found in her car on the side of the road after the night of violence that brought an end to Greg Grom. She was in possession of the preserved remains of the Union Island Blue Octopus—the last specimen known to exist. She had just stolen it from the island museum of natural history. She had made a mistake handling the specimen with her hands and experienced a massive dose of the toxins from the specimen. According to our records, she was declared dead and was buried within twenty-four hours in a Union Island grave."

"Must have been faked."

"Not necessarily, Remo," Smith said. "The toxins in question are known to cause complete paralysis, including decreased respiration and heart rate. In the aftermath of the incidents on the island, it's not unbelievable that a careless physician failed to check a body adequately for signs of life. There were many dead that evening, if you will recall."

"Yeah, it was a real mess," Remo said. "So you think that part of the story is true? Well, hold on to your boring old fedora, because it just keeps getting weirder. First of all, Smitty, she said that when she came out of the grave and figured out she was still alive, she had some sort of revelation or something that told her to start her little religion and name it Remo."

"There must be more to it than that," Smith insisted. "She was hiding her real reason."

"She wasn't lying, Smitty," Remo said. "I don't think she knows what she's talking about. I don't know if she knows much of anything. This is one seriously messed-up young lady. But she is also teamed up with some seriously strange individuals. And now it gets even *more* weirder."

Smith asked sourly, "'More weirder'?"

"Just listen. She calls these guys 'acolytes.' I thought an acolyte was a little Christmas candle that smells like cinnamon. I haven't found out who these guys are or where they come from, but they might be the ones behind the whole thing. They all look like they had skin diseases and they don't talk much, but they have some of the strangest metabolic mechanisms I have ever seen. Their heart rate is steady as a clock and their breathing is unnatural. They also seem to have the ability to climb trees quickly."

"Climb trees quickly?" Smith said.

"That's what I said, Smitty. When I was on the way to the village I saw one of these guys jump around in the trees like a monkey. Like some sort of Tarzan."

"Perhaps they are, in fact, trained monkeys," Smith said.

"They talk, too," Remo said. "They also kill. Just after I got here, there was an altercation out front between the one of the villagers and one of the staff members. I got the impression that it was Dawn Summens's personal assistant who had ticked off one of the villagers. A guy named Rohrman. The villager freaked out and snapped his neck, then ran into the swamp. One of the acolytes ran after him, and I'm using his phone now."

"The villager was Joey Wild?" Smith asked. "He is dead?"

"Dead does not begin to describe it. This guy had his leg pulled off. They tied a rope to his leg and pulled it very fast. The leg is now hanging on a tree nearby. The villager died on the ground. It's easy to figure out where, because there's a bloodstain about twenty feet in diameter. But then they took him up in the trees and left him here and that's where I am now. Funny thing is, his phone is still working.

"I don't know what to make of this, Smitty,"

Remo said. "The whole situation in the village itself is strange, but not strange enough to keep me interested. The acolytes are something else. I don't understand what they are. There's something about them that is just not normal. It has to be them manipulating this whole situation. I just can't figure out why."

"Yes," Smith said.

"That's your cue to come up with some lamebrain explanation for it all and then back it up with a bunch of mumbo jumbo from the computers," Remo explained.

"There is much that is unexplained here," Smith replied. "We must assume that anything involving Dawn Summens probably involves use of the same mind-control drugs that caused the Union Island incident. Remember how Greg Grom caused many deaths when he experimented with synthetic versions of the drug on his tour of the United States."

"Sure, I remember. Those people were insane. But not the way Dawn Summens looks insane now. Besides, Greg Grom became shark food a long time ago."

"Summens's accident came about from mishandling the specimen that contained the toxin. We can assume she knew of it and was taking it for her own uses. If she's alive, her mental state is most likely the result of brain damage in that incident. But we must assume the mind-control drug is still a factor in her plans." Smith seemed to be thinking out loud. "But Greg Grom was not, perhaps, the brains behind the scheme on Union Island in the first place. His records and profile do not point to a huge intellect. Dawn Summens is less of a known entity. She did exhibit extreme cunning. If I recall correctly, you had an entire lunch with her and were not able to determine if she was involved or not. Clearly a duplicitous mind."

"Clearly," Remo said. "Where's this getting us? It doesn't make sense out of anything here in the Big Haiti Swamp."

"Perhaps you should keep the phone belonging to Mr. Wild for use in the future," Smith suggested carefully. Remo was notoriously uncooperative when it came to carrying personal communication devices.

"I'll give it a try, Smitty," Remo said. "I am not making any promises. This has got more buttons on it than Mark has on his computer. It took me fourteen tries just to get a call through. I'll stash it away here in the tree where I can get at it again if I need it. How's that?"

"I would prefer that you carry it on your person," Smith suggested.

"Now, we both know that isn't a good idea. It will just get smashed or lost or who knows what."

"But I could track your whereabouts," Smith said reasonably.

"That I *don't* need."

20

"He could not have gone to the body," said Tree-top Man.

"And why not?" the young woman demanded. "What makes you so certain?"

"I placed it high up. So high, the branches could barely support its weight. So high that no other man could climb to it. The tree would not support them."

"Look for him," Dawn Summens said, turning to Jar Carrier. "Tell me what you see."

"It is too far," Jar Carrier answered.

"Try."

Jar Carrier shuffled his feet, but he reached to the clay pot that hung on a strip of hide around his neck and twisted off the wooden lid. He dipped his fingers inside and raised them to his face with a dab of gray grease. He touched his fingers to the outside of one eye and pulled the grease across the eye, across the bridge of his nose and across the second eye.

Then he turned in a slow circle, gazing around the room.

"I do not see him."

The small, bent, mouselike man with the blood-red eyes wiped his palms on his coarse, hand-stitched garment. "Try better!"

"I do what I can do," Jar Carrier snapped. "I am seeing as far as I can see!"

The young woman turned on the little mouselike man, who was wavering and staring at his feet.

"You can do it," she said to the little mouse of a man. "You can see if he's there with the dead one."

"It makes me ill."

She laid her hand flat across his face. He bent and clutched at his head, whimpering.

"See him!" she insisted.

"Yes, mistress." The little mouse of a man raised his head and promptly sprawled on the floor of the chamber, lifeless.

REMO TUCKED THE PHONE into a crook in the tree and became aware that he wasn't alone. There was someone below. He could feel their eyes on him. But Remo couldn't see them.

He looked in the trees. It must be Treetop Man. He must be back, perched far away and watching Remo through the branches. But there was nothing.

But Remo could feel it. Eyes were on him. He had acquired the ability to sense it, and though he didn't have this skill developed to the level of his mentor, Remo could tell when he was being watched. And there were eyes on him now—but where *were* they?

They were the eyes of the corpse. Remo knew it suddenly. The corpse of Joey Wild lay there with its eyes wide open, lifeless and motionless, as it had been since he'd found it, and yet, its eyes were looking at Remo.

Remo stepped to another branch some distance away from the corpse. It was as motionless and dead as it should have been. There was no sign of movement or nervous activity or circulation, and yet the eyes were seeing him. Remo controlled a shiver of unreasonable fear and stepped along the tree branches until he had the trunk of the tree between himself and the corpse—and the sensation went away.

"HE IS SITTING in the tree," squeaked the voice of the little mousy man from the limp body. "He sits in the tree with the liquor man. He knows he is being watched."

"Who is watching him?" the Priestess demanded.

The little man reported, "Me. He senses me inside the body of the liquor man. It makes him afraid."

"It is not possible."

"Nor possible that he clings to a tree that cannot support his weight, and yet it is so."

"He is more than you know," said Leatherhead.

The young woman narrowed her eyes at Leatherhead. "What do you mean by that?"

"Just as I said."

"And what do you know of him?" the young woman asked. "What do you know that you do not tell?"

Leatherhead raised his hands palms up.

"Once again, you give me no answer!" Dawn said. "What see you now?"

"He is leaving the body," the mousy man said, and came back into his own body with a shudder of revulsion. "He left. He is gone."

"Look!" Dawn ordered Jar Carrier. Jar Carrier was moving his head as if trying to see around things.

"Go get him," she ordered.

"He would not leave the village," Leatherhead said.

"You do not know that!"

"There's no need," Leatherhead said.

Dawn Summens turned on him. "*I* say! Not you!" She turned on Treetop Man. "Catch him." And to his silent companion she said, "Help him!"

The pair rolled their eyes at Leatherhead. They were looking for guidance. Leatherhead said nothing, but the young woman brought her hand across their faces.

"Listen to *me!*"

They cowered and scrambled out the door.

HAROLD W. SMITH skimmed through the archived records of the troubles on Union Island—specifically, refreshing his near perfect memory as to the nature of the poison used on the island.

The Union Island Blue Ring Octopus was well known from the writings of the unusually literate Miytecs, who were the original settlers on the island. Both the Miytec people and the Union Island Blue Ring were extinct now, surviving only in the form of mummified remains.

The Miytec records told how the Union Island Blue Ring Octopus had great ritualistic value to the people. For one, it was used to test the mettle of a new holy man. If the young initiate caught one of the octopi without being stung, it was a sign that he was worthy to be a leader of the people. If he was stung and died, he wasn't. There was no record of a middle ground—no one ever was stung and survived. The poison, received in a natural dose, was simply too virulent.

This strange, extinct subspecies was a variant of the smaller Blue Ring Octopus that survived to the present in many of the world's oceans. The surviving Blue Ring had a poison of its own, but it was the traditional and widely studied tetrodotoxin, or TTX. TTX was found in puffer fish and other marine life, and was infamous for being the active ingredient in Haitian zombie potions. TTX poisoning from consuming the wrong parts of a puffer fish was frequent enough for there to be an established medical procedure for it—though it was rarely successful if more than a fragment of the poison was consumed.

The poison in the Union Island Blue Ring was not chemically identical to TTX. The lab that tested its molecular structure dubbed it guaneurotetrodotoxin, or GUTX. The lab said it was an interesting molecule, but not a *very* interesting one. It wasn't likely to be chemically or biologically reactive in any unique way; in fact, the cases of GUTX poisoning that occurred from the careless handling of desiccated octopi specimens gave researchers every reason to believe it would act almost exactly like TTX.

In other words, there was no research interest in the further study of GUTX.

The labs were bribed heavily to report this finding.

The one who bribed them was an expert in Miytec

writing and had studied GUTX in the extensive Miytec literature. Union Island Blue Ring Octopus essence, made from the dried, ground remains of the creature, was administered by the Miytecs to certain victims in very tiny doses.

The man who read this literature, Greg Grom, had confirmed that the old writings were accurate. GUTX made strange work of certain parts of the human brain, essentially turning off specific mechanisms of ego and making the victims entirely suggestible.

Grom tested the theory by suggesting some things to a very pretty girl who hated Greg Grom. His suggestions worked. The very pretty girl willingly did what Grom asked, although she had been repulsed by him not long before. Extensive testing on many pretty women confirmed the efficacy of GUTX.

Greg didn't stop with pretty women. He used his supply of GUTX on a lot of people. He used it to convince them to elect him Union Island president. He convinced them to aid his companion to make Union Island an independent entity from the United States, but still financially supported by the United States. Grom became very rich.

Grom's power play nearly worked—except that his supply of Union Island Blue Ring Octopus essence ran out. There were only so many dried-up octopi to grind into powder and now they were gone.

He needed another source for GUTX, but there was no other natural source. That was when Grom began ordering, and performing reckless human testing with, various synthesized formulations of GUTX.

The testing caused Greg Grom no end of problems, which eventually spun out of control, and Greg Grom abruptly dropped out of sight.

21

Remo knew when he was being followed. He heard the movement in the trees, and he knew what it was. It was Monkey Man. The one who flew from limb to limb. That was strange enough.

What his fear told him it might be—that was even stranger. And it wasn't true. But he kept thinking about the vivid sense of consciousness that he had sensed in the body of the slain Joey Wild. What *was* that? What of Joey Wild was pursuing him now?

He made himself a shadow in the trees and allowed the sound of his pursuit to close in. His fear was a palpable thing. What had him so damned spooked? He had seen strange things before. Crazy, insane things.

There was even more to it than the fact that a dead man had been staring at him. There was more to it than Monkey Man, who swung in the trees. What was it that had him so scared?

There was a flight of movement in the trees. It was Monkey Man, just as Remo had known it would be. Monkey Man sprang across the distance between one tree and another and clung to a swaying mangrove branch. Peering into the woods. Looking for Remo.

Remo drifted like a ghost through the branches. Monkey Man might be faster than Remo in the branches, but he made every leaf rattle. Remo was silent, as he went on the pursuit.

Monkey Man bounded from tree to tree, and a dozen times Remo was almost upon him when Monkey Man would fly away again. It took an hour for him to finally sneak up and place his hands on Monkey Man.

Monkey Man grunted, but before he could make another noise he was pinned to the twisted trunks of an ancient mangrove. Remo held him hard, cutting off his breath until the brown, hideous creature stopped squirming. When he released Monkey Man, he gasped for breath and shrieked abruptly.

Remo applied pressure on his neck again, and Monkey Man twisted and struggled until he was ready to pass out from lack of oxygen. When Remo let him breathe at last, he didn't have the will to shout again.

"Let's talk," Remo said.

"A messenger comes for you," Monkey Man croaked.

"When?" Remo asked.

"I am the messenger," said another voice, and Remo turned on the high branch to find another acolyte standing at his back. He had the presence of mind to snatch the second acolyte by his neck, and he had a freak in each hand.

In that instant, Monkey Man made a tremendous leap toward the sky.

Remo felt the move coming, and he wedged one leather shoe deep in the twisted branches of the mangrove. When Monkey Man sailed up, he lifted Remo up with him—only to have Remo pull him back down and send him crashing into the second acolyte. The impact should have shattered both their bodies.

The acolytes hung in Remo's hands, limp and broken, but they were alive.

He carried them back to the Priestess of the Dawn and flung them at her feet.

"What are they?"

"My acolytes," Dawn Summens said.

Remo couldn't figure her out, either. She was contained, subdued, but there was something big inside of her, trying to burst out.

Remo Williams was afraid of her, too, he realized, but he wasn't the kind of man who ran from his fears.

"You know," he snapped at Leatherhead, "you're one of them. What the hell are you? What's Monkey Man? What's this one?" He shook the limp creature that had sneaked up on a Master of Sinanju. In a tree.

Nobody should have been able to sneak up, ever, on a Master of Sinanju.

Leatherhead spit the words. "You know we are *sadhaka.* Gifted with the *siddhis.*"

Remo dropped the acolytes. "I don't know any such thing."

But the words registered with him, making his fear grow. What did those words mean? It must be some old lesson of Chiun's. Why hadn't he paid better attention to Chiun? He was in grave danger—that he knew—but what was the danger?

"You know me," Leatherhead said.

Remo said, "The power of *khadga.*"

The power to turn swords. Where did those words come from? What did they mean? Had Chiun taught him the words once?

"See if it is true," Leatherhead taunted. "Slash at me with your pathetic Knives of Eternity. See them be turned aside."

Leatherhead bared his chest, daring Remo to slice it with his fingernails, which were tough as steel and sharp as razors but scandalously short by Sinanju standards.

Remo forced the dare away. He was missing something. Leatherhead was trying to distract him from—what?

There was the agitated Priestess and the semi-conscious Monkey Man and the sneaky acolyte and there was—another.

The little, mousy acolyte was cowering away from him, and something in Remo's minds came out. *"Parapurapraveshana."*

The little mousy man stopped cowering and made a shrill laugh. Remo backed away. He had to run away fast; he didn't know why but he knew he had to flee. Then the Priestess slipped forward and snatched his hand.

"Not yet, my love."

The mousy man plopped to the floor, a boneless mass, and then Remo Williams felt someone else in his head.

THE ONE CALLED Drunkard, the acolyte with *parapurapraveshana,* found himself looking out through the eyes of the consort and felt the movement of the consort's mind. It was the normal reaction, when the mind seeks to retreat from the utterly new experience of having another mind occupying the brain space. Drunkard had felt it a thousand times. Sometimes, simply putting himself into the minds of his victims was enough to send them reeling instantly into the abyss of insanity. Sometimes they simply shut down their consciousness as a way of escape, leaving Drunkard the freedom to use the body however he wished. Others fought back, and Drunkard knew the consort would be a fighter.

The consort regained his mental composure in an instant, and pushed back against the intruder in his head. It was a mental battering ram. An exceedingly powerful mind. This was going to be painful, Drunkard thought. He shoved back against the mind of the consort, and the two consciousnesses grappled for dominance of the body.

"Control him," said the commander of the servants, the one the villagers called Leatherhead.

"Trying," croaked Drunkard, through the lips of Remo Williams. At that moment Remo's hand slashed viciously across Leatherhead's chest. He left only a long, harmless white scratch, but the force of the blow cracked Leatherhead into the raw stone wall.

Drunkard strained for control against a mind that seemed to gather more strength at each passing moment. To him it felt as if he were struggling to balance a massive barrel on his shoulders, even as more water poured into the barrel. Even his gift of sight was incomplete, causing the vision of the Priest-

ess's chamber to swell and narrow by the moment—
and seeing through the eyes of his victim was the
purpose of *paraprapraveshana*. When had he ever
wrestled with a mind this powerful?

"Control him!" the Priestess commanded.

Drunkard forced his mental body to inflate inside
the mind of the consort, and for a moment only did
the consort lose his grasp, then back he thundered
into the battle, pummeling the mental body of
Drunkard, squeezing the spirit air out of him.

Drunkard lost his senses and was dizzy, while the
consort seemed unable to get his mind wrapped
around his physical body again, and the body of the
consort went to its knees in the Priestess's chamber.
The acolyte with the power of *khadga,* with the skin
like toughened hide, pushed his shoulder into the
consort's back to send him toppling to the floor. The
consort's hand's snatched Leatherhead—even while
the mind still seemed unable to control the body—
and Drunkard was horrified when the consort's
hands spun the head of Leatherhead around on his
neck. The bones snapped. The skin twisted and
stretched and became light, and Leatherhead collapsed. The Priestess wore a look of horror.

Drunkard knew the payment for his failure. Suffering and suffering and every moment that his failure continued, his punishment would increase a

hundredfold—but what could he do? He was only so strong and the consort was of a strength unimagined.

"Immobilize him! Just a moment is all that is needed!" The Priestess held an amber clump of congealed, transparent spheres. The mass was as big as a large egg.

Drunkard released all the power that was left in his mental body and he visualized himself pounding the consort's consciousness like a berserker. The consort was overcome. Drunkard summoned every ounce of spiritual energy and kept the consort subdued until he felt the physical body hit the ground. He delighted when the tunnel of his vision through the consort's eyes widened. He was in control of this supreme body.

The Priestess thrust the amber glob between the teeth of the consort. "Bite!" she commanded.

Drunkard felt movement on either side of his spiritual self. The mind of the consort was swelling with anger and *there was another!* and they sank their claws into Drunkard's spiritual consciousness and tore him apart. Drunkard's last spiritual vision was something red and blazing in the blackness of the consort's mind.

"BITE DOWN!" the Priestess ordered.

The eyes were rolling back in the head of the

consort, as if the *khadga* acolyte was engaged in battle again. Then the physical body of the *khadga* acolyte twitched. The small mousy man opened his eyes and out of his mouth came a rising howl of horror.

The consort grunted and launched himself through the door and was gone.

"No! You will stop!" The Priestess was in hot pursuit, and she didn't have to go far before spotting him stumbling in the trees. He wiped his arm across his face, then bolted deeper into the mangroves as if in fear of her, and sought safety in the top branches.

"Remo, you will obey. Come down now," the Priestess called up to him.

The consort nodded and flopped down the twisting branches, ripping his T-shirt and landing on his backbone bent over a root. The Priestess watched the consort rock on his shoulders, as if the battle continued until the eyes sprang open, blazing with red fire—but almost immediately she relaxed. Amber fluid was smeared across the consort's mouth, and the coals behind his eyes burned to the color of cool ash.

"Remo?"

"Wha'?"

"You will listen to me now."

"Why?"

He sounded drunk. The Priestess was concerned. The dose in the gelatin tablet had been massive. What had possessed her to give him that much gua-neurotetrodotoxin?

She had known somehow that he would be difficult to subdue, even with the GUTX. How had she known this? She had shaped a mass of tablets in her hand and wetted the mass, and it had hardened into a solid clump of individual gelatin tablets. But how many doses had been in there? Twenty? Thirty?

She'd expected some of them to be lost. But it looked as if the consort had ingested most of them, losing no more than a trickle of amber from the corner of his mouth.

"You will listen and obey," she announced.

"I will?" Remo mumbled.

"You will. Stand up."

The consort rolled onto his hands and knees and pushed himself slowly to his feet, then swayed on his knees.

"You belong to me now," stated the Priestess of the Dawn. "Do you understand?"

"Yes."

"Say it. Tell me you belong to me."

"I belong to you."

"You live to obey me. Say it."

"I live to obey you."

"You will answer all my questions. You will keep nothing from me. Say it."

"I will answer all your questions."

"Starting now," Dawn said.

"Starting now," Remo agreed, his eyes closing and his head rolling on his neck.

"First question," she said. "Who am I?"

"Dawn Summens."

"No. Who am I really?"

"Priestess of the Dawn."

The consort looked as if he might pass out. Christ, the GUTX was going to put him under, or kill him. Why had she given him so much of it? "Remo, listen to me and answer!" she begged. "You must tell me who I am! Please!"

The consort said, "Dawn Summens," before he dropped to all fours and fell flat on the earth.

No answers. *He was supposed to provide the answers!*

There was no sound in the swamp except the sobbing of the Priestess of the Dawn.

LEATHERHEAD FOUND the scene pathetic. He hoped his commitment to this Priestess of the Dawn would soon end. He made much noise when he came to

them among the trees, so they would not know he
had witnessed the scene.

When he reached them, and bowed, the Priestess
had dried her tears. "Bring him."

Leatherhead moved tentatively, and the Priestess
asked, "Did he injure you?"

"No, Priestess." This was a lie. His neck hurt. It
would hurt for years to come, if past experience
served.

"Why do you fear him?"

"I do not fear him, Priestess." Another lie.

"He cannot hurt you now. He's trapped in living
death."

The acolyte shuddered at the thought of the consort being aware, at this moment, of all that was
going on around him. This was not the kind of poison with which he was familiar—and yet the
Priestess herself had fallen victim to it, once. Shud-
dering still, he lifted the body of the consort and
carried him back to the stone chambers of the
Priestess.

Every moment he touched that flesh was a nightmare. Was the consort listening and feeling and
knowing what was happening to him now? Did he
feel the hands of the acolyte bearing him? Was he
trapped in his own mind with nothing to keep him
occupied except his awareness?

Leatherhead flopped the consort onto the bench in the chambers and moved away, sickened.

Even to monsters, there were such things as monsters.

22

The doctor was honored to be called to perform a service for the Priestess, only to find there was nothing he could actually do to help her.

Dawn Summens looked apprehensive, which made the doctor's heart want to break. He loved his Priestess more than anything else in the world. Nothing mattered more than her well-being. "I don't even know what the poison is."

"Tetrodotoxin."

"Tetrodotoxin?" the doctor gasped.

"I told you. From fish."

The doctor was dreadfully sorry that he had never had a case of tetrodotoxin poisoning during his years of practice. He hated to let the Priestess down by showing his ignorance.

"It is too late to purge the toxins. You said you administered treatment? What kind of treatment, Priestess?"

"Charcoal capsules."

"Good. That should help absorb some of the toxins," the doctor said.

"Twenty-five at 260 milligrams each."

"That's appropriate for some kinds of toxin ingestion," the doctor said, trying to remember his ER training.

"I tried administering injections of neostigmine and edrophonium. The needle failed to penetrate the skin."

The doctor racked his brain on those. "Why did you do that, Priestess?"

"They're used to restore muscular strength to victims of tetrodotoxin intoxication."

"I see. Did you say the needles wouldn't break the skin?"

"I also tried an intramuscular injection of 4-aninopyridine."

"Four-aninopyro—what?"

She snatched some glass bottles from a table and slapped them in his palm.

"But what's it for?"

"It's a nondepolarizing neuromuscular blocking agent. They used to use it for multiple sclerosis treatment. It's been shown in animal testing to reverse tetrodotoxin toxicity."

"I see."

"Irrelevant, since I couldn't place the needle intramuscularly. You try it."

The doctor, mystified, filled a new syringe from his own medical kit and jabbed it into the upper arm of the patient, only to watch the needle bend, leaving the arm merely scratched.

"Doesn't seem heavily calloused," he murmured, then tried another spot. The third time he used his strongest needle. It turned into a fishhook instead of penetrating the arm of the patient.

"Is there *anything* you can do here?" the Priestess demanded.

He murmured, miserably, that there was not. "You've already done more than I would even have known to do."

"Then get out. You're not to discuss this with anyone."

When the doctor departed, the Priestess called for her acolyte—the one called Leatherhead. He had another name, but at the moment she couldn't remember what it was, and she didn't care.

What she did know was that he was afraid of Remo, her consort. This was strange; the man was in a coma, probably on death's door. He couldn't be more helpless. Leatherhead wasn't afraid of anything.

Anything except Remo. Even now, Leatherhead

took up an uncharacteristically humble posture, behind her and at a distance from Remo's couch.

"What is this man that makes you act like a fool?"

"I do not know his nature."

"He is the key to my identity!"

"I know nothing of him."

"You know he is more than a man. You have seen what he can do. Where is his companion?"

Leatherhead shuffled his feet, disturbed in a new way. He, too, was more than a normal man, and yet the beauteous Priestess was not as enthralled with him as she was with this Remo. This angered him.

What was he thinking?

Could it be that he coveted the flesh of the Priestess?

He almost laughed out loud at himself. He was a fool to allow his thoughts to traverse that path.

"Heed my question!"

"There is no companion," the acolyte said.

"An ancient man, Asian, small. He is known to dress in Asian robes. He is not in the village?"

"He is not."

And yet, the flesh of the Priestess was worth coveting. She was a creature of unrivaled and arresting beauty. Her skin was perfect and dappled with highlights. He had rarely seen a female with freckles and never bedded one. Her hair was polished like spun dark copper, yet soft to the touch. Her shape was slim and called for hands upon it. The Priestess seemed heedless of the effects of her body on her acolytes— because it didn't even occur to her that they were men.

But she stirred them, even her loyal acolytes, with her provocative flesh.

Leatherhead chided himself that she was but an infant to a man as old as him! And he hadn't bedded a woman since before the Priestess came into the world! He carefully resurrected his shameful memories. There had been so many times when the stirring in his loins had led him astray of his purpose and made him look like a fool. He cared nothing for the women whom he had violated; it was the derision of the others that finally drove him to be celibate.

The urge had been his constant obsession for years, for decades, until it began to fade away. For so very long now he had gone without the pleasure of the female. How sweet it would be to partake of it again! Rather, how satisfying.

It would not be like tasting an old favorite food, so much as it would be finally scratching an ancient itch.

Old fool! He should not even allow the thoughts to linger in his mind. He was still a hostage to his urges, even after years of denying them. But they had never gone away. There was simply nothing to call them up during the long years since they had gone into seclusion in the hovels behind the temple on the other side of the world. Now all it took was stimulation from the Priestess to bring the impulses to the surface again.

THE PRIESTESS SENT Leatherhead to fetch the little man. The man begged in the most unseemly way, but in the end he relented to the will of the Priestess.

"Extract the knowledge of his companion," she ordered.

"I will try."

The little man fell in a heap on the floor.

The body of the consort twitched. The consort parted his lips.

The little man with the *parapurapraveshana* became conscious again, but he was led away screaming like an animal. Whatever he found in the consort's mind was unbearable to his psyche.

But the end result was just as well for Dawn Summens when she saw Remo open his eyes and sit up on the cot.

Leatherhead was fighting the urge to flee, but the Priestess didn't notice. "Remo. Can you hear me?"

"Yes."

"How do you feel?"

"Bad."

"Touch your nose."

Remo put his finger to his nose.

"Stand up."

Remo struggled to get to his feet, then fell back on the cot.

"Good, Remo. Now, tell me where to find your companion."

"What companion?"

"The one that came with you to Union Island. He is a man like you, is he not?"

Remo opened his mouth. He was showing his clenched teeth. Then his teeth came apart as if with great effort and Remo said, "Yes."

"What is the name of this man?"

Remo's jaws seemed to creak from the strain. "Master Chiun."

Leatherhead was aghast. That this man could come to his senses again—and struggle against the will of the Priestess—was unthinkable! No human being could fight the Priestess's will. Did the Priestess not see the struggle and understand the force of will this man exercised to refrain from answering, even though he failed?

The Priestess cared only that she got her answers.

"Master Chiun?" the Priestess asked.

"I am his apprentice."

"I see," she said.

It was a half truth by the one called Remo; the Priestess failed to see the obfuscation. Leatherhead was not so blind.

"Where is Chiun?"

"Piney Point Beach Retreat, Site 14B."

"I have never heard of this place," the Priestess said, foolishly oblivious to the deceptive nature of the consort. "Tell me more about it."

"It is a campground."

"In the United States."

"Yes."

"Where."

"South Carolina."

"Where, Remo?"

"Near Myrtle Beach."

"Good enough." She leaned into the consort and kissed him on the forehead, which was damp with perspiration. She didn't know what an extraordinary thing that was. Even Leatherhead didn't realize the significance of a little sweat—that it came from tremendous exertion.

"Watch him. Alert me of any changes."

Leatherhead cursed her in his mind, but answered, "Yes, Priestess."

She left him with the hated consort, the one who struck fear in his heart. The one who had felt the touch of her lips upon his flesh. Leatherhead reviled the consort with all his being.

THE PRIESTESS FELT ENERGY in her limbs such as she had not known for as long as she could remember. She stood before the front of the ruined stone mansion and peered into the chinks between the bricks. Even her eyes must look in the cracks in the walls and the shadows among the weeds to find Sandal Wearer.

There he was, where there had been no one a moment ago. He was standing against the wall, in his own mind.

He was the most enigmatic of the acolytes. Was he thinking vast, wise thoughts, or simply daydreaming idiot dreams? She didn't know if he was a simpleton or demigod. She cared only that he was obedient to her.

"Sandal Wearer."

He was startled out of his reverie as if he had not noticed her presence. As if she had been the one camouflaged in broad daylight.

"Priestess?" He bowed his head.

The acolytes had come to her when she had just arrived at this place in the mangrove preserve. She couldn't recall them ever asking her for her leave to join her. It was as if they had always been with her. All her life. But it had been little more than a year. Sometimes it occurred to her to wonder where they came from, how they came to be so strange—but the interest quickly faded. In her months with the acolytes, she had interacted least of all with the one who served as her messenger boy.

"I have need of you at last, Sandal Wearer."

"I serve you, Priestess. I shall run like the wind to deliver your word. To whom do I carry your instructions?" Sandal Wearer was an emotionless husk of a rail-thin man. Every word he spoke came across as lip service.

"You go to find an ancient man—one more wrinkled by time than yourself. He may be a dangerous man. You will watch him. Nothing more. Report to me of his actions every other day. He is called Chiun." She gave him the campground address.

"Other instructions?" he asked.

"None. Take your leave."

The camouflage seemed to spread over his skin until the Priestess found herself staring at the wall where Sandal Wearer had been. He would already be on his way to find the one called Chiun.

SANDAL WEARER had been a normal boy until the day when he was fourteen and sought shelter from the rain in the Temple of Aruvi, where the Holy Mother was worshiped.

In truth, he and his friends, many boys from the area, had not come to worship. They were on the hunt for an attractive low-caste girl, and they had money to pay. Not much, but enough to earn the services of an unclean low-caste girl. The trick was for one of their number to give her money, earn her obeisance, and get her to come of her own volition to a private place where she might perform her service. In that private place the other boys would come forth and take their pleasure, as well. It was a harmless diversion. No such girl would cause them trouble; even her father would forbid her to make the issue public.

This was the kind of entertainment the gang often sought out. They were notorious in the district for their crimes and their impunity—they came from important families.

To see the entire gang enter the temple on that day put fear in the hearts of the other worshipers. Who knew what trouble they might cause, even in a holy place?

The day didn't turn out the way the boys planned. Although they had not come to the temple to visit the Holy Mother, the Holy Mother was there for them.

The boy that Sandal Wearer had once been dropped to the floor of the temple and felt his consciousness replaced with the consuming presence of the Goddess. It was like being a water skin filled so much that the seams strained. He remembered little of the orders she gave him.

When he found himself returning to the real world, there was mayhem in the temple. He learned that all his friends had fallen senseless at the same moment as he—and most of them were dead.

"Slain by the Goddess," exclaimed the enthusiastic priest. "They were evil ones, but you five young men had better hearts. You experienced the *maha-bhava,* the all-consuming love of the Goddess!"

All-consuming, yes—love, no. To the boy of fourteen, the love of the goddess felt more like shackles. His free will was subverted to a new desire—to serve the Goddess above all else.

He and his friends were treated like heroes by the people, and they were brought in as interns to the priests of the temple, and years later when they were grown men, the Temple of Aruvi came under their administration. And the years came and went without meaning.

The one named Rajara was their ceremonial leader, and it was he who brought the five boys, now graying men, into the private chamber of the Goddess deep inside the temple. He said the Goddess asked him to bring them.

Here, the five were struck down again with *mahabhava,* and came back to their senses a short time later to find the statue of the Goddess changed. She had taken on new features—non-Tamil features. An infant's features. Almost European.

They also found themselves in possession of the *siddhis.*

For the one who would come to be called Sandal Wearer, his *siddhis* was the sandals that would let him run forever—and the first time he tried to use them, the violence of the run nearly shook his body apart.

He took up the training of his body that would let the sandals have their way with him. There was no thought of discarding them. The unwelcome compulsion to serve the Goddess had never faded.

All the others continued to be held in the Goddess's thrall. The five boys had grown into morose men, prone to silence and brooding. All were afflicted with the stiffening of the skin as if they were sailors exposed to salt spray for all their lives, not priests who dwelt in comfortable shelter with decent food.

The others practiced with their *siddhis* in secret,

and waited for the next communiqué from the Goddess. More years came and went and at last it seemed the call would never come. The only sign of her presence now was in the infant statue in the dark chamber. The face changed. It became a girl, and then a striking woman. Thirty more years were lost.

The one who was now Sandal Wearer found entertainment in his old, pre-Goddess ways, using his new Goddess-given skills of distance running and concealment in plain sight.

He would lope overland for hundreds of miles, then creep into the home of a rich man. He would stand in a room to watch the private affairs of the family, and test how close he could get to them before they sensed his presence.

Sometimes he pushed too far. The alarm would be raised and he was chased out of the house. Great manhunts would be staged in the vicinity of the rich man's house, but Sandal Wearer would quickly be far away, back at his home in the temple.

As his skills improved, he found he could walk with virtual impunity through mansions and palaces. Into banks and places of business. Into markets and merchant houses. To hone his skills further, he set about stealing items of fantastic wealth, although he quickly tired of taking riches that the Goddess prohibited him from spending.

The Goddess cared nothing for the women who were Sandal Wearer's victims, so he began taking the richest and most high-profile daughters of the region, one after another. Into their bedrooms he came like a phantom, unnoticed by guards or surveillance systems, to truss them and have his way. The families rarely reported the assaults.

Once only was he caught. A spunky girl, newly betrothed, worked a hand out of her bonds as he was upon her. She snatched up a poison barb that all the women were now keeping bedside, and drove it into his flesh. He awoke bruised and beaten in the cellar of the family home, but concealed himself in the shadows the first time the heavy wooden door was opened. His keeper entered and found the cell was apparently empty. The house came alive with activity, and Sandal Wearer slipped away easily.

He took no further chances. When he returned to that very house days later, he made sure the bride-to-be was helpless before he finished his long-interrupted pleasure taking. She strangled in her ropes.

They all did, and the district was in a panic, and the Goddess at last took notice of Sandal Wearer's entertainments. She sent him pain. When he ignored it, she sent more pain, until at last Sandal Wearer was persuaded to cease the slaughter of the daughters of rich men.

It was back to the low-caste girls. They didn't fight his visitations, and so they survived. They didn't even complain to the authorities. Sandal Wearer became a legend among the working girls. To be visited by him was good luck.

As he and all the others aged, they began to debate, furtively, the option of passing on the *siddhis* to younger counterparts. They were approaching old age. It was inevitable that the afflictions of old age would begin to take them soon enough.

But the inevitable had not happened, and finally the elderly priests began walking with bent backs and trembling hands to fool the outside world. They returned from service and cloistered themselves and waited.

Sandal Wearer felt the years as a heavy weight on his soul and prayed to the Goddess to make use of them or to make an end to them. Then the call came, from around the world, and the five old men who had been boys left the country of their birth and came to this miserable, alien place where they found the Priestess of the Dawn, with the same face that had been etched upon their Goddess effigy in the temple for the past thirty years. The Priestess was driven by madness, and was as cunning as a demon and in possession of an earthly power as great as their own powers bestowed by the Goddess. She used the power to assemble a flock, but with no real purpose. She sought to create an earthly paradise for her flock, but it was based on superficial, transient pleasures. None of it was based on the teaching of the Goddess temple—nor on any of the schools of religious thought. It only pretended to be derived from the chaotic worship of the people of the island. The Priestess of the Dawn seemed to have developed a pointless form of worship.

"My aim is to be known far and wide," the Priestess of the Dawn said offhandedly once. "In that I am succeeding."

She was indeed. The people came to her village to live a life of worry-free hedonism. Word spread. More came. From North America and Europe, even from Brazil and Japan. The village numbered in the thousands. The Priestess's inexhaustible funds supported them all. There seemed to be no meaning to it, but the loyal *sadhaka* continued to serve the Priestess of the Dawn, finding their purpose in the rare glimpses of the Goddess who spoke through the mad girl's mouth during her wild ceremonies. The Goddess said they must assist the Priestess. The Priestess did the work of the Goddess.

So they served this comely, mad child as best they could, and waited for the Goddess to make her purpose known.

23

The phone rang fifty times. Then it stopped. Five minutes later it started up again and rang fifty more times.

Then stopped.

Piney Point Beach Retreat had once been a thriving beachfront camping getaway, but went belly-up years ago. The land was now in the hands of a new owner. He leased out parcels on a less than formal basis, provided no amenities and gave his guests all the privacy they could ask for.

The guest at Site 14B had paid his fee for a year in advance. His younger companion had come to the owner's trailer on a separate occasion and paid to lease nine other sites—this was after there was trouble with some other guests, who had apparently fled in the middle of the night. To avoid further trouble, the younger man said, he wanted to be sure none of the other sites in a close proximity to 14B were rented out again. Ever.

The owner was more than happy to take the younger man's money.

So now, when the phone in the gleaming, restored Airstream camper at 14B rang 450 times over the course of several hours, there was no one to complain.

The resident of the camper was deep in meditation, and he was not annoyed by the sound of the ringing. It was as inconsequential as a mosquito buzzing on the other side of a paper screen.

The man was in the meditation chamber at the back end of the camper. It was a pleasant environment, secluded and peaceful. The camper was a thirty-foot Airstream Sovereign of the Road, half a century old but perfectly restored to mint condition.

Chiun found a kind of peace in his old travel trailer. It was as close to peace as he seemed to be able to achieve these days. Subtle, unpleasant thoughts were gnawing at him. Questions he could not yet answer and uncertainties he could not control.

Was he ill? Remo seemed to think he was. Remo based his diagnosis on the reactions of the illness-sniffing dogs that had been used to cut down on medical expenses by an insurance company. Chiun and Remo had encountered the dogs—and the dogs had clearly reacted as if they detected a disease inside of Chiun.

Chiun meditated through the entire night, listening to the signals of his body, looking for some signal that he had missed thus far.

The Master of Sinanju Emeritus finally sensed something out of place—and it came not from within, but from without.

Chiun rose and glided to the phone as it started ringing again, turning off the sound, then listened further.

There was something in the woods around the camper that should not be there. It was so quiet even he could not identify it, hearing it just enough to know it was an alien presence. It wasn't natural, because Chiun was familiar with all the sounds of these coastal woods and this was strange. It wasn't another human being, because no human being could stay so quiet and be so close to the Master of Sinanju.

Chiun repaired again to the meditation chamber and descended gracefully into the sitting stance of his meditation. Whereas before he had sent his senses inward, exploring his own body for a sign of infirmity, now he allowed his senses to drift outward, beyond the aluminum skin of the Airstream, into the woods, probing the weeds that grew in the sandy soil, listening for what should not be.

Chiun found it.

CHIUN'S SINANJU SKILLS allowed him to move about
the creaky metal trailer every day without causing it
to shake or squeak or groan, and now he used even
greater stealth as he sneaked through the vehicle and
made his exit by slipping through a rectangular window over the kitchenette counter. There was no sound
or sign of movement as he drifted under the trailer and
crept out alongside a wheel, where his movement was
masked by low plants and moon shadow. Then the old
Master slithered among the growth like a serpent, although with less noisy scraping of scales on sand.
When he was a hundred paces into the sparse tree
growth he finally allowed himself to stand and begin
his long journey around to the far side of the Airstream.

All this stealth would have been overkill if the
watcher in the woods was human. Chiun was convinced he was not. He breathed with human lungs,
to be sure, but breathed less than thirty times in an
hour. Even the greatest yogis—whose ancient pred-
ecessors acquired much of their knowledge from
careless Sinanju Masters—could not sustain respiration that slow and remain conscious.

Chiun was faced with either an exceptional sleeping yogi in the woods, which was unlikely, or an unknown Sinanju Master, which was impossible, or
something else.

But what? Chiun would err on the side of caution until he had the answer.

He reached the position in which he had placed the cause of the noise directly between himself and the Airstream, and then he began to close the gap. His care paid off. After some fifty paces, he spotted the human-shaped figure among some young pine trees. The figure faced the Airstream, standing stock-still with his arms stretched above his head, his hands fanned out. The pose made the man's silhouette look remarkably like the other trees. Chiun was impressed that the man could hold the pose. It required much stamina.

Chiun came closer, and clearly heard the continued, measured breathing. Chiun lowered into the soil in a sandy place, some ten paces behind the figure, and waited.

He would take the measure of this creature.

If he was the extraordinary camouflagist that Chiun suspected he was, then dawn might motivate him to change position. As the secluded corner of Piney Point campground became lighter gray, the figure in the trees shifted his position. Down to the ground he went with barely a whisper of sound, maintaining perfect balance to his weight at all times. Maybe he was some master yogi, Chiun allowed.

And Chiun knew precisely why a master yogi would stalk the Master of Sinanju Emeritus.

The figure slunk backward on all fours, until he was but an arm's length from Chiun, and then he raised his front end, drew his legs beneath him, and became still among a copse of sparse sand grasses. They were as high as a man's waist and most dense in the place the stalker had hidden himself. A breath of predawn breeze swayed the grasses almost immeasurably—and Chiun was amazed to see the visible top of the figure's head sway with them, in perfect harmony.

"Your skills are admirable, limb bender, but you are a fool to think they are sufficient against me."

The creature pivoted his head slowly, staying in his cover.

"Even now you maintain your cover, under the chance that my words are broadcast about, to flush you out. Yours is a true talent that will be disappointing to destroy."

The creature met Chiun's childlike hazel eyes, and knew he was found out. He sprang out of the grasses with a wasteful flurry of sand.

Chiun gave chase, and was amazed again as the creature's speed continued to climb. Faster he went in a gait that was not so perfect as his slower, stealthy movements. It was as if his feet moved with fantastic energy and his body flopped along with it as best as it was able. Soon enough, if he kept going faster, he would move more quickly than Chiun could pursue.

The old Master bore down on the creature and snicked at his feet with his longest fingernail, which severed the sandal straps as if they were webs of spun sugar. The sandals flopped off his feet and the spy tumbled end-over-end as the two of them emerged on the South Carolina beach.

The figure sat up, shocked to find his sandals gone, and scrambled over the sand on his hands and knees in search of them. He was slow to realize that Chiun was standing with him, the sandals in his hands.

The figure spoke for the first time, but his voice was a soft hiss like the hush of outrunning surf. "Give those to me. You know not what they are."

"Paduka Siddhi," Chiun said.

The creature buried his face in the sand, shamed and afraid.

"You have been gifted with *siddhis,*" Chiun said. "Who are you that you know such things?"

"I shall ask the questions. You are a worshiper, a *sadhaka,* but whom do you worship?"

The *sadhaka* ran again, but without the sandals he ran no faster than any normal man, and Chiun brought him tumbling into the sand again after two steps.

"Whom do you worship?" Chiun repeated.

"The Priestess of the Dawn."

"I am not familiar with this Priestess. Where can I find her?"

"In her enclave among the ancient mangroves on the isle of Hispaniola."

Remo was on Hispaniola. The existence of this creature took on worrisome connotations. "You are not a yogic spy sent to steal more Sinanju secrets."

"Sinanju!" the creature hissed.

"Is not the Priestess but a cultist capitalizing on the voodoo mysteries? Answer me."

"Yes."

"There is more to her than you know?"

"Yes!"

"Who gifted you with the *siddhis*? Was it the Priestess of the Dawn?"

"Yes. No!"

Chiun had the creature then, flipping him onto his back and holding him down to the beach sand with his fingers poised to bore into his heart. "You will answer!"

"It was her, yes, the Priestess! It was her flesh that called to us from around the world. We came to her in the mangroves. We found her forming her worship. We did not understand how she came by the power to call us. But it is during the feasts when the Priestess overcomes her strength and surrenders her body and then we speak to the Holy Mother."

Chiun understood.

The *sadhaka* misinterpreted the horror on Chiun's face. "I speak only the truth, great Master of Sinanju! The Holy Mother delivered us our *siddhis*."

"Describe the *siddhis*, each of them!" Chiun's finger bore down on the tough flesh of the strange man.

"The *anjana* is one. Mixed with rendered fat and smeared upon the eyes."

"To let one see through the walls and the trees and earth," Chiun said.

"Yes. Another is *khadga*. That one has skin like tough hide."

"To turn swords," Chiun concluded.

Sandal Wearer nodded. "Another one of them has *khecari*."

"He leaps into trees, up mountains, almost flying," Chiun said.

"The last of us has *parapurapraveshana*."

Chiun said, "Ah. The power to possess. And what has been accomplished using this power?"

Sandal Wearer said, "Entrapped the consort."

Chiun's worst fear was realized. "The Goddess is finished with you."

Sandal Wearer couldn't believe the words. "That is all? My whole life in preparation, for this one failure?"

Chiun was not sympathetic. "You chose a poor path."

"I did not choose! I was chosen—"

Chiun worked his Knives of Eternity into the chest of Sandal Wearer and removed his heart. For good measure, he took it with him, to one of the other occupied campsites. There was a despicable man who lived in a wooden structure in the bed of a pickup and fried foul food on an iron skillet that was never cleaned. Chiun knew this simply from the smells that wafted to his own campsite when the wind blew in just the right way.

The despicable man was snoring in his truck bed, with his grungy socks protruding from the rear opening. His fire from the night before still smoldered, and Chiun waved his hand at it to feed it a steady stream of oxygen. In seconds, he had coaxed dancing flames out of sleeping coals. He put the heart of Sandal Wearer into the fire.

This was probably unneeded, but he could not know the true nature of the being with the *siddhis* sandals. It was best to reduce the heart to something that could never again be used. The heart steamed, and finally shriveled in the heat, and then was only a black husk, and Chiun was nearly beside himself with impatience.

He feared the worst for Remo.

He feared the worst for himself and for them all.

When the heart was turned to char, Chiun hurried back to the Airstream.

24

He turned the volume back up on the blinking phone and the bleat commenced at once.

"Emperor."

"Master Chiun?" Smith said. "I've been calling all night. Remo is in trouble."

"Emperor Smith, we are all in much danger. We face the enemy that will defeat Remo one day. It is Kali."

"No. It is Dawn Summens. The Union Island minister of tourism. Remember her?"

"We never met."

"She and Remo met. We believed that she was in collusion with Greg Grom. We suspected she might even have been the brains behind some of his more audacious moves."

"I recall that she was said to have died, when all the others died on the island," Chiun said, but the pieces of the puzzle were falling now into place.

"She was found in her car, in possession of the last preserved Union Island Blue Ring Octopus, and declared dead at the scene from GUTX poisoning. But the GUTX is said to be capable of causing the zombie syndrome. Decreased pulse and extremely shallow breathing. It could be she was affected. She told Remo she was buried alive but somehow disinterred herself."

"You spoke to Remo?" Chiun said.

"Two days ago. Then nothing. What has me concerned is that Remo reported strange activity by a group of Dawn Summens's acolytes. He claimed they were abnormally gifted with certain skills. He was going to investigate further. He was also trying to get Dawn to talk sense. Specifically, as to why she named her cult after him. Remo reported that she exhibited erratic behavior. She's likely emotionally scarred by her experience on Union."

"There is more to it than that, Emperor," Chiun reported. "She serves as an avatar. All that happened, the fact that Remo found her comely, her ability to use her potions to warp minds, made her at once powerful and suggestible. She is being exploited by Kali."

"Kali?"

"The reason she named her famous cult after Remo is simple—to bring Remo to her. The reason she made the cult at all is easy to answer—to spread its name across the country and bring it to Remo's attention. The gathering of worshipers will give Kali strength as she seeks the impetus she needs to break free into this world."

"Master Chiun, I think the explanation may be less spiritual in nature," Smith said in a sour, condescending tone. "Keep in mind the schemes of Greg Grom on Union. He was after a power base and a source of wealth. That's precisely what Dawn Summens has seized for herself on Haiti. She's virtually untouchable by the U.S. or the UN. The Haitians love her because she's bringing in tourist dollars for the first time in years."

"All this is a part of the mechanism. There is but one purpose to it all, and that is to ensnare Remo, the avatar of Shiva the Destroyer."

Smith was silent for a long moment. "This is the old Armageddon story, Master Chiun."

Chiun was stiff in his reply. "What I believe is more than fairy tale, and discarding my explanation would be unwise, Emperor," Chiun said. "The Divine Mother, Kali, is perpetually eager to mate with her lover of old, Shiva the Destroyer. It is the impulse she cannot deny, and she long ago surrendered to it."

"Yes," Smith said quickly, but got no further.

"Kali knows that in the mating she will serve as the Shakti of Shiva, giving him the power and the impulse with which to destroy the world."

"I don't quite see how Remo will destroy the world," Smith interjected.

"Time and again, this particular avatar of Shiva has denied her the fulfillment of her compulsion. Remo is already her prisoner."

"What? How do you know this?"

"One of her acolytes visited me," Chiun said offhandedly. "Kali chose her avatar well. Remo had feelings of passion for this Dawn Summens. She will entice him to taste her womanly charms and he will not resist her. Kali bides her time and waits to enter her own avatar when the mating is under way and the ending is inexorable."

"Why do you believe this has not happened already?" Smith asked.

Chiun sniffed. "Because the world goes on as before."

Smith challenged him further. "Remo is not easily held captive. How could she do it?"

"She has befuddled him."

Smith betrayed his shock. "Guaneurotetrodotoxin."

"There are many reasons this human woman makes an ideal tool with which to ensnare Shiva the Destroyer," Chiun said. "I will go to the mangrove swamps now. Send your roaring aircraft at once."

"They're standing by approximately fifteen minutes from you. They will pick you up on the beach."

"I will be there. Emperor, I know you do not believe in all that I am telling you. And for once, it does not matter. There is nothing that can be done by you, except to transport me swiftly to the place and hope we are not too late."

"I can accept that, Master Chiun," Smith said. "But what is it that you will do to save Remo?"

"I know not," Chiun admitted, then hung up and headed for the beach.

25

The young man was on his way home from the southwestern United States to New York state.

He had mixed emotions about leaving. This was not his favorite part of the country, and the project he was involved in had a particular, unpleasant physical effect on him. He had constant headaches, joint pain, nausea. It was like being hung over day after day. Finally, the physical toll became too much.

Dr. Harold W. Smith ordered him to leave the facility. "You are clearly not effective there any longer, Mark."

And Sarah Slate ordered him to leave. "You're killing yourself and you're not much help, honey."

Mark agreed with their assessment, but he hated to go away from Sarah. "You'd be alone here. With *him*."

"I'm not alone," Sarah said. "There are doctors, nurses, patients."

"And none of them know the full story."

"It's one of the most secure military hospitals on earth," Harold Smith reminded Mark Howard. "There's no reason to think our friend will find a way to escape. And I need you here, Mark." He did not elaborate.

It wasn't him escaping that Mark Howard worried about. It was him hurting Sarah Slate, his fiancée. Sarah was with the prisoner every day.

The worst part of it was that when he left her there, he had no idea when she would be leaving. Her baby-sitting with the prisoner was an indefinite assignment.

Now that he was miles away from the military hospital, he had a new outlook. The headache was already fading and his stomach had stopped churning. He strolled through the terminal feeling like a new man.

Then his phone rang. It was Smith on an encrypted satellite call. Oh, God, something had happened already. Smith was calling to tell him to head back to the military hospital at once. Sarah was hurt, or worse.

"Yes, Dr. Smith? What's wrong?"

"I have a change of plans for you, Mark," Smith said sourly. Mark liked Smith, but sometimes the director of CURE was as cold as a human being could be.

"Is Sarah okay?" Mark demanded.

"Yes, Sarah is fine. This has nothing to do with Sarah or the prisoner," Smith explained.

Mark Howard moved the phone away from his mouth and exhaled long and low.

"I need you in St. Thomas. I have booked an itinerary for you. You must connect in Miami. You have three minutes to catch your flight."

Mark Howard got the gate and set off in a hurry, without even knowing what it was all about.

26

The smell was what woke him. It was the aroma of burned pork, and damned if his campfire wasn't blazing away. Most days when he woke in the morning he found nothing but a few warm coals. There was something in the fire, and whatever it was made the smell. It looked like a lump of meat.

He scratched his pits and grabbed his cook pole, which was a rod of extruded aluminum that used to be the trim on the back wheel-well of his pickup, but when it came off he found he could stick wieners on it for roasting. He batted the chunk of meat out of the fire and stared at it.

It looked like a heart. There seemed to be arteries sticking out of it, all burned up now. Maybe some sort of an animal had got into the fire accidentally and was roasted spontaneously. Didn't seem likely, but where else could it be from?

One thing for sure: it was too burned up for him to eat for breakfast.

He was just opening a can of potted meat when he saw someone coming toward his campsite. A little man, but with a big, big opening in his chest.

The thing in the fire was a human heart and it belonged to the little man. These two facts were now undeniable, no matter how much sense they didn't make.

The man sent the half-open can of meat flying at the zombie.

"Stay away from me!"

The man who owned the heart wanted it back, and as he crouched over his charred heart he made a mournful sound and picked it up—then he looked hungrily at the camper.

The camper knew somehow what the little zombie wanted.

"Stay back! It's mine."

The camper was obese and slow, and he didn't get far before he was clubbed to the ground with the very piece of extruded aluminum he used to heat up hot dogs.

It turned out the attacker didn't want to take the camper's heart, just the camper's blood. He bathed the burned heart in the blood that flowed from the open neck of the camper. The camper lived long enough to see the restorative effect his blood was having on the incinerated heart. The flesh was being nurtured and the tissues were becoming soft. The damage was being undone.

Long after the fat camper lost consciousness the blood continued flowing from his neck, and then the heart in Sandal Wearer's hands throbbed. Sandal Wearer thrust the organ into his chest again, then basted the pit with more of the camper's blood.

Somehow the stranger's blood gave his tissues the nourishment they needed to attach themselves to his body, and soon the perfectly circular opening was covered over with pink, new skin.

Sandal Wearer felt his strength returning, and his instincts took him away again, into another part of the campground. This was a much nicer camper. His instincts told him to break the door and enter. He did, and found his sandals, placed neatly in a closet. He tied the slit straps and put them on his feet.

He found a fish in the refrigerator. Now two days old, but still palatable. He devoured it, then left the place and walked down the shoreline, feeling strength seep into his muscles.

He was alive again, but it wasn't the same kind of life. His skin felt grainy. His blood felt unclean. This was a temporary reprieve from death, at best.

His new purpose was unknown.

Soon he felt the sandals eager to run, and run he did. Across the miles. Across the states.

He took a route down to the very end of the southern peninsula of the United States, then followed the bridge spans out into the Keys until the land ran out and he took to the waters.

He toppled into the sea ten times every hour. He wasn't the runner he had once been, and he rejoiced when the solid ground of Cuba was under his sandals. He traveled the length of it on foot, losing track of the passage of days. Finally he stepped on the water again, and struggled a day and a night to traverse the Windward Passage.

Then his sandals walked on the solid earth of Haiti, and he began the final run across the blighted country to the mangrove preserve on the south shore, and to the Priestess of the Dawn.

He didn't know what he would find when he arrived there.

27

Mark Howard had fifteen minutes to rendezvous with the courier in the terminal in the Miami airport, then make his connection.

The courier was just in from the northeastern U.S. and held out a fingerprint scanner. Mark Howard passed the scan and a briefcase was handed over to him.

Mark Howard snatched it and jogged to make his connection.

Only then did the courier realize his scanner had gone black. The damn thing was smoking! It was hot! He tossed it from hand to hand as he headed for the men's room, just barely getting it into the sink before his fingers started sizzling from the heat. He ran cold water on the device until the smoking stopped.

Ruined. He wondered how something so small could get so hot. The memory card looked like a ridged potato chip and it came out of the slot in pieces.

One thing for sure—there wasn't going to be a record of the fingerprint scan of his drop-off.

The courier hoped that would not be a problem.

MARK HOWARD WAS ON the ground in St. Thomas past business hours, but the private postal box storefront allowed all-hours access. Using the key from the briefcase, Mark let himself inside, then used another key to open Box 144. It was the jumbo-size mailbox, allowing delivery of packages such as the one that waited inside from a chemistry lab in Oregon. It was plastered with Chemical Hazard stickers.

Howard placed it the counter and slit the tape, removing the contents carefully. Five sealed vials of shatterproof plastic. Warning labels said they were to be opened by authorized chemical technicians only.

Mark Howard wasn't about to disobey the warnings. He opened the briefcase, which also contained plastic vials, and swapped them out, one by one. His replacement vials looked nearly identical. The only difference was the batch serial number, and even that was a close approximation.

He covered the slit tape with fresh tape and put the package back into the postal box, which was rented out to one Dawn Summens.

28

She had no choice but to travel personally to St. Thomas for the latest delivery. Typically she entrusted Sandal Wearer with this duty, but he was away on other business.

There was an irritating urge to postpone the trip, at least until after the next ceremony—which made no sense, since the ceremony couldn't work without the shipment that was waiting to be picked up in St. Thomas. She fought against the distracting urge.

Sometimes she felt like two people, and one of them was a pest with bad ideas and a big mouth. When these thoughts came into her head she tried to ignore them and push them away. Other times they were too strident to ignore.

But this time she had her own way. Leatherhead steered her boat out through the shallows of the mangrove preserve and into the open waters of the

Caribbean, where the floatplane was waiting at daybreak. It was her usual pilot, and he had her in the air in no time. St. Thomas was an easy five-hundred-mile hop. They were landing in the Charlotte Amalie harbor before lunchtime.

She stepped onto the dock in her civilian clothing. Khaki slacks. A cotton shirt. Canvas deck shoes. It had been ages since she had dressed in clothes that the outside world would call normal, and they were absolutely foreign to her now. They tightened around her body, compressing her chest and abrading her skin. She stepped hurriedly up the street of the little city to the storefront where she rented the post box. She let herself in, grabbed the package and stormed out again.

Her flesh crawled. She broke into a jog when she reached the dock and she ran to the floatplane. The hired pilot was surprised to see her again so soon. When Dawn Summens snatched the door open and dived into the aircraft, he leaned in after her.

"What's the matter?"

Dawn Summens stowed the package and kicked off the shoes. She yanked the shirt over her head.

"Are you hurt?"

When she had completely divested the repellent attire, she answered him, "I am fine."

"Did something happen? Should I call the police?"

"Nothing happened. I am ready to return home."

"Oh. Okay."

As the pilot taxied away from the dock, he said, "There's a blanket in the back bin."

"I prefer to remain as I am."

The pilot preferred she remain as she was, too. His instrument panel gave him a reasonably good reflection of his attractive nude passenger. He was sneaking glances of her all the way back to Haiti.

29

Leatherhead rowed the narrow boat to the door of the floatplane and held it steady for the Priestess. His face didn't show that he noticed her nakedness, but he did notice. His body stirred in response.

The Priestess parked her bare behind on the wooden bench. She wasn't even looking at him. As far as the Priestess was concerned, her acolyte was not a man. She could be as shamelessly exposed to him as she could to a pet. "Get me back to the *hounfo*."

It annoyed him, her use of the local words, all of them false. *Hounfo* meant something like the holy congregation in the village, but it was one of the words of the voodoo tradition.

He had served as a priest of the Goddess for a long lifetime, and even for one as faithless as he was, the traditions had sunk into his being. The voodoo affectation of the Priestess was ugly to his eyes.

Certainly it made some sort of sense to adopt

some of the traditions of the religion of this island, since her church was here, but did she have to use the words, even when it was just the two of them?

The Priestess was grandly naive. She knew not what she did. She knew not her purpose. When full understanding came, she would forget all her gaudy voodoo trappings and her petty disdains. But would she forget that she had disdained her loyal acolyte?

In fact, she would disdain him all the more, for then she would be a goddess, with her beautiful consort, and would have no use or desire for Leatherhead.

Ah! He was thinking of himself in the name the villagers gave him in their whispers. But it was more meaningful than the name he'd had when he was a boy. Leatherhead was the name of a freak in a sideshow, and that was all he was.

But was it all he had to be? Could he break free of the compulsion that had chained him to the Goddess's will all his years? Could he escape? Could he take his talents into the world to find his pleasure?

Could he even take some pleasure here, in this place? Surely the Goddess would strike him down when he was no longer useful, and that would be very soon. Maybe, before the Goddess came, he could taste of the vessel the Goddess had chosen.

For his eyes had trouble moving off the lithe and temping flesh of the Priestess of the Dawn.

Dawn Summens turned her gaze around the boat, and for a moment Leatherhead was terrified that his thoughts were open to her, but she was looking into the trees. She never even rested her eyes on him.

SHE BENT OVER the cot of her senseless consort and summoned her acolytes. "Have you heard from Sandal Wearer?"

"It is too early, Priestess," Leatherhead explained. "He is due to report tomorrow."

She made a face. "Have you seen him?" she asked the tree-climbing man, who had the gift of *khecari.*

"I have not."

Her voice became harsh and animal, and she bent her knees, with her hands in claws. "Something in the trees!"

"What is in the trees?" Leatherhead asked.

"Something to make one afraid!" Then she stood again and pulled metal rings onto her arms and a scarf over her hair, her movements languid and calm again. "You will protect me, you strangers?"

"You know we will, Priestess."

"I know nothing," she said with playful gentleness. "Who are you? Why did you come? What's your purpose? You don't have a snappy answer for me now, Leatherhead?" She was almost playful and the acolytes didn't know what to make of it. This was disturbingly alike the Dawn Summens who was here when they came to her, more than a year ago. This Dawn Summens had become submerged in the Priestess of the Dawn.

"We are your servants," Leatherhead suggested.

"Jesus protect me from servants like you!" She laughed haughtily. "I see the images in your mind, Leatherhead. Is that the kind of service you wish to render on your Priestess?"

The acolyte could neither speak nor look at his companions.

"Answer me, please," she trilled.

"No, Priestess."

She stood before him, then took his hand, moved it to her neck and laced his fingers around her throat. He was frozen in fear and shame when she said, "This is the image in your mind when you dream of me?" With his hand simulating choking her, she opened her limbs, lewd in her nakedness.

It was, indeed, the very image that floated in his mind's eye, perpetually.

She laughed at him, stepped away and carelessly pulled on her voodoo-queen uniform, then said, "There is something in the woods. Find it. Protect me."

30

Chiun came to the little inlet where the boat had entered the mangrove swamp after taking on the unclothed young woman from the floating plane. He followed an open waterway deep into the oldest trees, stepping first on a gnarled branch, next on a floating clump of seaweed and next on the water itself.

His sensitive hearing picked out the sounds of activity ahead. It was men walking, trying to be stealthy, and one of them was coming his way. Chiun waited on a tendril of mangrove root for the man to come closer.

Chiun heard the man stop suddenly. He saw something.

He saw Chiun. Chiun could feel the eyes on him and yet he could not see the man. There was a call from the man and he came toward Chiun, bumbling among the roots and slogging in the water, and a second man approached from another way. Chiun slipped across their path, with no more sound than the dapples of sunlight. He would never be heard.

But again he was *seen.* Chiun's highly attuned senses felt the indefinable pressure in the ambient that told him there were human eyes on him. The clamor of the approaching men turned his way—coming inexorably toward him.

Chiun let them come.

BUT ONLY ONE MAN emerged from the mangroves, with a dour face and his flesh like the tanned-hide flesh of Sandal Wearer—only more stiff. Chiun could read the tick of surprise.

Even standing on a high root, Chiun was no taller than a child and his ancient, narrow limbs looked frail in his colorful Korean robes. His head was nearly devoid of hair, except for the tufts of yellow over his eggshell ears and a few yellowy threads on his chin. His hands were inside the sleeves of his robe, and he appeared infinitely calm even in the face of danger.

"You are not the one who sees through the trees," Chiun announced in a singsong voice.

But Leatherhead didn't respond. He simply came to Chiun and pounded his fist hammer-like on the wrinkled, ancient head. His fist whistled on empty air and Chiun was now standing on another root, a few paces away. Leatherhead came to him and snatched at the twiglike arm.

"What are you?" Chiun asked, now on the far side of a sea of twisted roots.

Leatherhead began to pick his way across the obstacle course, muttering curses from his childhood.

"You call me a dog in excrement, when it is you who allows such filth to come from his lips?" Chiun chided in the same Tamil dialect.

Leatherhead twisted around to find that Chiun was now where Leatherhead had started from. "You are not one of my people!"

"And this is something for which I am grateful."

Leatherhead bounded over the roots with all his speed, which was considerable. No man could outmaneuver him. He struck into the soft, fleshy part of the old man's throat, only to find the throat moved aside, and then a powerful blow struck his shoulder.

Leatherhead staggered but didn't fall.

Chiun put his own foot into Leatherhead's shin, which only pushed the foot out from under him. Leatherhead recovered himself, but Chiun struck with one finger into Leatherhead's temple. Leatherhead's head ricocheted from the force.

Chiun examined his own throbbing finger and Leatherhead stared at him, clutching his rattled skull.

"What are you?"

Chiun held up the backs of his hands with his fingers erect, displaying the gleaming fingernails and the one exceptionally long, exceptionally deadly, nail on his smallest finger.

"Another Master of Sinanju!" Leatherhead said.

Chiun nodded and stepped into him, slashing his nails across Leatherhead's chest and joints. If he had been a man, his flesh would have been shredded and his arms and legs lopped cleanly off. But Leatherhead looked down at nothing more than a crisscross of white scratched in his flesh.

Chiun bowed at his handiwork. "The power of *khadga,* making you invulnerable to swords."

"And to the Knives of Eternity! Now we see what you are made of, old man."

Leatherhead grabbed at Chiun and found the old man had not escaped him this time. He locked his hands behind the old man's back. He sensed the lightness of the bones. It would be like snapping twigs! And he crushed the little body into his own hard flesh.

The bones didn't break, but then the hands of the Master of Sinanju were pressed against his eyes, rubbing them with uncanny speed. The friction became intense. Leatherhead dropped him, but Chiun stayed with him and Leatherhead felt his skin begin to sizzle from the heat. There was a sickening stench of burning flesh. Leatherhead turned and ran, but tripped at once on a root and went to the ground. The little palms were back on his face, rubbing him and burning him and cooking his eyes in their sockets. Leatherhead tried to throw him off, but then the hands were on his mouth and nose, and the rapid-fire friction began to sear his nostrils closed and his mouth was welded together in the intense heat.

Leatherhead grabbed his own mouth and wrenched his flesh apart and made a loud, long moaning sound.

Chiun snatched a thin, leafy branch from the mangrove and wadded it in his hands. The great force compressed the branch into a pellet, which was inserted into the open, lowing maw, which Chiun slammed shut. The branch began to open violently without the huge pressure, but Chiun had already used the friction of his hands to weld the flaps of flesh together again.

He couldn't penetrate the ensorcelled flesh but he could damage it just the same. He snatched a hand of the one with the power of *khadga* and passed it through a mangrove root, then clamped it across the fused mouth, ignoring his struggles, and moved the hand rapidly until it became heated and cauterized into one mass of flesh.

He couldn't remove the heart from this one, but the smoldering thing that remained was blind, gagged, unable to breathe and imprisoned by his own welded leather skin to the deep roots of the old tree.

Chiun could feel the eyes of the watcher on him. The entire battle had been observed. He took to the trees and slipped with speed that would make him too fast for human eyes to follow—even, perhaps, for the inhuman eyes that were observing him.

31

The unclean old man snatched the stopper from the jar and prodded his fingers inside, then smeared more of the rendered fat on his eyes. He turned around, then turned back, peering into the sides of the nearby trees. With a small grunt he started back through the mangroves to the village.

He didn't get far before he felt the most curious lightness on his being. When he looked down, he found the thong around his neck had been cut.

The ancient Asian man was on a tree branch nearby, peering into the clay jar.

"That belongs to me! You dare not take it!"

The truth was, he had not been without the jar on his neck in thirty years. The first time he'd put it on, it had locked on his neck. When he attempted to remove it, the hide adhered to his flesh. He had battled the jar for months, before surrendering to the inevitability of wearing the unpretty necklace for all time. Now he could not bear to be without it.

"The Goddess will strike you down! She will eat your heart! *Give it back to me!*"

Chiun sniffed the jar gingerly. "Why must you mix your *anjana* in filth? It is putrid."

"It is mine!"

"What animal have you not rendered the fat from for this concoction, *siddhis?* Even the blubber of a man is in it."

"It disgusts you, so give it to me!" Jar Carrier was now breathing and leaping madly in place, his mind unhinged by the loss.

"It must be made clean," Chiun announced reasonably, and snatched a peg of dead wood from a leafless nearby branch, then twirled it between his thumb and fingers with the end grinding against the rough pottery side of the jar. The stub of wood smoked, then glowed, then burst into flame.

"I dislike using tools, but sometimes a tool is needed to accomplish extraordinary deeds," Chiun explained. "Fire makes a good tool for cleaning that which is unclean."

Chiun put the little flame into the pot, careful to allow none of the foul unguent to touch his flesh. The fat flamed up and sizzled in the pot. Jar Carrier said some word, but it extended so long and high it became a howl.

"There is more to be cleaned," Chiun pointed out. When the wailing Jar Carrier came to his senses, he saw Chiun holding the flaming pot in one hand, and he was extending the finger of his second hand. Jar Carrier looked at the finger.

While Jar Carrier's eyes were wide open, Chiun splashed the burning fat on him, and Jar Carrier screamed again. His eyes burned. Chiun stepped through the air and landed on Jar Carrier's shoulders and delivered a kick to his chest that flopped him on the ground on his back. Chiun stomped on his hands as he attempted to grab his burning eyes. The skin was tough and the bones were like iron rods but they broke under the light sandals of the Master of Sinanju. When Jar Carrier was helpless, he poured more of the flaming fat across his eyes. The vitreous jelly boiled and the eyeballs burst, then the remaining tissue fried in their sockets. Chiun filled the little hollows with dollops of burning fat until the jar was finally empty.

Still, he tended Jar Carrier and his precious jar until the fire had no more fuel left to burn. The clay pot held nothing but black, crusty char. The eyes were open pits in the moaning head.

Then Chiun clapped the pot between his hands and sprinkled the fragments among the woody roots.

Then he left the still-living thing where it had fallen.

In Chiun's mind were the images of the *siddhis* that were described to him by the one who came to him at the Piney Point campground. The one at the campground was gifted with sandals that allowed him to run vast distances. The one with the skin that could turn away sword blades had the power of *khadga*. The one who saw Chiun even through the mangrove trees had the *anjana* gift, mixed in the rendered fat of human and beast.

There were two more *siddhis* Chiun had not encountered.

He didn't think he would have to wait for long.

32

The mangrove forest was made up of thousands of smells, and when the village came near there were thousands more—human smells, plastic smells, food smells, body smells. But there was another aroma that didn't belong.

Chiun followed it until he came to a certain mangrove tree that was just like the others. He stepped up the branches to a small bole. There was a wad of amber capsules, melted and massed together and lodged in the crook of the tree, and around it, in the soft wood, was a set of curious, shallow cuts in the surface, the wood smoothly punctured and showing the cast-in striations of fingerprints. They were the indentations of Remo's pathetically short fingernails.

The repulsive mass of amber capsules, from which flowed amber oil, was the source of the odor. Chiun knew that odor. He had smelled it before, or something very similar, and the odor confirmed the fears of Emperor Harold W. Smith. It was the smell of a poison from an animal that died out long ago.

Chiun had smelled the poison that came from the desiccated remains of the extinct Union Island Blue Ring Octopus, and he had smelled more than one laboratory-made synthesis of the same poison. To his sensitive nostrils, the poison in the amber fluid was clearly another man-made concoction, but it was closer to the natural poison than the other synthetic versions.

The purpose of the poison was to enslave the one who ingested it, because it made the victim completely suggestible to the one who exploited it. The man-made versions of the poison had come with virulent side effects—driving people mad and turning them into mindless killers.

Chiun sat on his tree branch and meditated on the meaning of the disgusting mass in the tree. That Remo had left it here Chiun did not doubt. No other creature or human would have left those marks in the tree, and no one save Chiun would be able to identify them.

Chiun could see no situation in which Remo would have needed to make such carefully executed marks in the wood save one: as a message. Remo wanted to make it clear to Chiun that it was he who had done this.

Remo had spit the capsule into the bole, as well, and Chiun understood all.

Remo had been forced to ingest this mass of poison. How this had come to be was mystifying but not impossible, given the powers of the acolytes of the Holy Mother. Remo would have known the smell, as well; no matter what trickery was used, the smell would have told him the nature of what he was ingesting at the moment the first capsule burst. Remo must have known the poisoning would soon make him helpless, and during the seconds of self-control left to him, he had deposited this unpretty present for Chiun. "Remo was here," the message said. Remo was poisoned, but Remo was not as poisoned as his enemies might think he was.

"Clever," Chiun admitted out loud in a voice as small and songlike as a swamp bird.

If ever he found Remo alive, and if Remo's mind could be saved, Chiun vowed he would tell his son what a cunning ploy it was.

He must go find Remo.

33

Chiun heard the sound of drumming as the night closed in on the village, and the night was bright with the flicker of a bonfire in the village. He approached with trepidation, and found the bonfire was in the Priestess's courtyard. He couldn't see in, so he stepped up the branches of the mangrove trees. These were easy trees to scale. Their tangled branches made them almost like steps.

It came as a shock when he felt the twinge in his side.

It was just below the bottom of his ribs on the right-hand side, where he had not felt pain before. It was an insistent bothersome pang, and it would not go away.

Chiun didn't have the time for it. He pushed the pain away. But the pain would not go away. As if it had come out of nowhere to become a fixture in his existence, the ache stayed there in his side.

But Chiun was watching the ceremony below in the courtyard of the hundred-year-old Haitian estate home. He was looking for Remo. Remo didn't seem to be about. Neither were the acolytes, but Chiun suspected they were nearby. They would stay close to their Priestess.

The Priestess was standing on the stone ledge of the fountain as the bonfire burned before her. She was swaying with the beating of drums, which were in the hands of her flock.

There might have been three hundred members of the village in attendance already. More were coming. They were whites, mostly. The Caucasian suburbanites of America, transplanted into the swamps of Haiti. There were a few with darker skin and even some Asian faces among them, but they were like the token ethnics in a white television program—they didn't change the nature of the flock.

Chiun was appalled and amused that so many of them had succumbed to the lure of the Priestess. It took little more than a well-produced television commercial to convince many of them to give up the lives they had built and run away to the swamps, simply for the lure of no responsibilities and rampant fornication. Some of that fornication, Chiun couldn't help but notice, was continuing in the shadows even during the worship ceremonies of the Priestess.

But why were they here? What was their purpose? How did they serve the Goddess—not the Priestess, Dawn Summens, but the creature that was using her. Kali.

Chiun didn't understand the ways of the gods. He didn't even feel hatred for the one called Kali. She was simply fulfilling her purpose, and who could say that the instincts of the Holy Mother were not in the best interests of the earthly realm?

But the purpose was catastrophic to Chiun's eyes, and he felt some kind of a responsibility to interfere. It was his adopted son who was the avatar of the one known as Shiva the Destroyer.

Kali was *devi. Devi* was nothing more, nothing less than the vast consciousness of the all-encompassing power that some called God. The very concept of Shakti was not understood by mankind—even by the wisest of men. Even by Chiun. He understood one thing only: what he knew of the purpose of the gods was beyond his understanding.

Therefore, he could react to the machinations of Kali as nothing but a human being—narrow of vision, shallow of intellect and entirely mortal.

Was not this human body even now showing its mortality? The pain in his side would not fade.

He watched as a group came forward with white paper cones, and began pushing powder out of the tips of the cone. They knew what they were doing. They had done this before. The people kept their distance from the growing lines that were formed by the spilling white powder.

The powder might be ground-up eggshell. Perhaps it was rice flour. The design began to take on the form of supernatural creatures and symbols. It was a *veve*—the complicated symbol of the voodoo god.

Or maybe it was the *kolam,* the Hindu symbols that also represented a voodoo god.

The Priestess was a stunning figure in her brightly colored robes, with swirls of red and yellow. Her head was dressed in a brilliant scarf of the same colors. Her wrists and arms were covered in bracelets and dangling charms, and the filmy skirts swirled provocatively around her legs, exposing more than they covered. Even in her trance she seemed filled with the energy of the heavens. She was truly the Holy Mother, and a more provocative figure Chiun could not recall seeing. How could any man resist the temptations of woman-flesh such as this?

Chiun watched for Remo to make his appearance.

Buckets of earth were carried into the courtyard

and dumped into the splashing fountain at the Priestess's feet until it was a pool of thin mud. Then the flock, man and woman alike, stripped bare to the waist and formed long lines to immerse themselves, twenty at a time, into the big fountains. Soon the courtyard was filled with earth-colored bodies. The drumming continued and the people began to dance.

The *veve* was complete. The dancers avoided it, but the priestess herself disrobed and bathed in the mud, then lay down in the middle of the *veve* and rolled about, covering herself with the power. Some of the shapes of the symbols adhered to her. This was no voodoo practice, nor a Hindu one. The dancing became wild.

Where was Remo?

The Priestess was swaying again on the edge of her fountain, and her hands gestured to the heavens gracefully and languidly. Then she sprang lightly to the top tier of the fountain, swaying still, and allowed the spraying water to cascade over her.

The effect on her flock was electric, who took their pleasure in each other, regardless of the mud.

And now the Priestess was the only one among them who was free of the earth. The water washed her clean and she was a pale, perfect figure of womanhood. She was a gleaming, polished marble statue. Her flesh caught the moonlight. Her hair clung provocatively to her flesh. Still she swayed and gyrated her fingers, then turned to face the tree.

"Join me in my worship, great Master of Sinanju."

Chiun didn't understand how she had known of him, but he wasn't surprised.

Her hands curled on her wrists, like the languid beckoning gestures of the great snakes. Her body language begged him to come to her.

Chiun watched her from his perch on the tree. He was stoic. Truth be told, he didn't feel stoic. The mystery pain in his side wouldn't fade. And he couldn't help but be affected by the performance of the Priestess. He was, after all, only a human being—and this night, he felt more human than he had in decades.

"A Master of Sinanju never fails to be man enough for any woman," the Priestess chided him. "And you are not so very old. And this body is ready for you."

Her glistening flesh reflected the firelight. With hundreds of worshipers gathered there, it was still as if they were alone, Chiun and the Holy Mother.

It was in this moment of distraction and temptation, when Chiun was allowing himself to wallow in the weakness of his humanity, that another acolyte struck at him.

"Old fool!" Chiun cursed in his mind as the trees exploded around him and something like an iron fist engulfed his body and Chiun felt himself rocketed into the skies.

34

Then the mangrove swamps came tumbling up to meet him again. Chiun felt the branches shatter against his body and he twisted to avoid the worst of them and snatched at the branches as he came down. The mangrove was stripped in a fraction of a second, but Chiun had used the branches to slow his fall. When he crashed into the ground he was up again in a moment—but the *khecari* acolyte was more swift. He was amazed when he saw that his victim was not dead and still had the presence of mind to snatch the little Korean under the arms and fly skyward again.

Chiun found himself sailing in the curious grip of the acolyte a hundred feet above the tops of the mangroves, then he was falling again, and as they came down Chiun slipped out of the grip of the acolyte and maneuvered him under his feet. He steered the acolyte into the ground. Chiun stepped off the plummeting body and into the branches to slow his descent. The *khecari* sprung up, unhurt, and sailed into the skies, and again he had Chiun in his grasp.

The acolyte was in a fury as time after time Chiun turned the tables. Still, Chiun couldn't escape the lightning-like rebounds of Treetop Man. Then they sailed up to find no more trees beneath them.

"If I cannot kill you I shall take you to the far end of the earth," the one with *khecari* wailed in an old Tamil dialect, and Chiun found himself skipping over the waters of the ocean like a stone skipping, but the energy that forced them on and on never dissipated. Chiun couldn't free himself from the grasp of Treetop Man.

It was a nightmare, but in it Chiun found calm enough to meditate for a brief moment. He assessed his body.

The pain in his side had vanished. The strength in his arms was as powerful as ever. He felt the change in the air and sensed land coming toward them. Their bodies slammed into the earth and the legs of the *khecari* propelled them into the sky again. They were in another kind of jungle.

Treetop Man carried Chiun for miles. Chiun was nearly boneless. Then, as they came down on a rising mountain, Chiun came back to life. Treetop Man had no time to react when he felt himself turned in the air. The stone came at them and collided with the skull of Treetop Man.

The creature staggered to his feet with his head smashed flat. He leaped impulsively into the sky, but Chiun grabbed him by the ankle and swung him into the stone again and again.

The thing wouldn't die.

Chiun broke hundreds of bones. Not a digit or a limb would function, and still the *khecari* didn't die. Chiun pounded the body until it flopped around like a collection of entrails, then he cracked open a place in the mountain with the kicks of his foot. He made a tight compartment and forced the body of Treetop Man inside, twisting and folding it upon itself.

If the thing wouldn't die, Chiun reasoned, then at least it wouldn't be able to cause more mischief for a while. It would need to heal and rebuild countless broken bones.

But stuffed into the little rock hole, the *khecari*'s bones would fuse in unworkable ways. If it had the strength to crawl out of the hole, it would crawl out as a crippled, deformed creature that could not possibly jump into the tops of the trees.

Perhaps, if fate was kind to it, it would find a way to break the healed bones again and begin the work of healing them properly.

Regardless, it would not be interfering with Chiun again soon.

The last thing Chiun did was find a boulder that was just bigger than the mouth of the narrow hole, and he stuffed it in, like a swollen cork forced into a narrow bottle.

MARK HOWARD PENETRATED the secluded, private chamber deep in the bowels of Folcroft Sanitarium. He was hit with a blast of cold air. The computer room was kept cool and dry.

The four mainframe computers looked old, but they had been upgraded so many times—mostly by Mark Howard himself—that they were now completely up-to-date in terms of their processing technology. Part of Mark's responsibilities included making sure the Folcroft Four stayed state-of-the-art.

Right now he was adding a dedicated subsystem—a special, tiny processor whose sole purpose was to generate the perfect sequences needed to open the encryption of certain new military computer nets. It was more computer access than a private hospital should need. It was CURE, of course, that would use the new decryption device.

Mark Howard was the assistant director of CURE, as well as the assistant director of Folcroft

Sanitarium. Mark had brought many attributes to CURE. He was intelligent, incisive and one of the best intelligence gatherers that Director Harold W. Smith had ever had the privilege to work with. Mark also had superb microelectronics skills.

When he got back to the office he shared with Smith, Mark announced his success. "The system should be operational."

Smith nodded and, without further fanfare, opened a connection to a supersecret medical facility in a military installation in the southwestern United States.

The data began pouring in.

Mark dialed a phone number. "Sarah? Looks like we're in."

"Good."

"How's it going?"

"As well as can be expected."

"Sarah," Smith said, adding himself to the phone call, "I assume you received the shipment from Mark?"

"I have the guaneurotetrodotoxin in a bio-chem safe," she said. "Except for the samples I provided the analysis lab."

"Good."

The call ended.

"God, I hate her being there alone with him," Mark announced.

"There is little alternative," Smith said.

"Dr. Smith," Mark asked, "what are you expecting to learn from the analysis on the GUTX?"

"We're running a comparative analysis of the molecular structure. You know that, Mark."

"But what will it tell you?"

"Very little," Smith admitted. "We know it's a synthesis, so the tests will only show us how it varies from the naturally occurring GUTX at a molecular level."

"But what we need to know is its effectiveness and safety when used on human subjects," Mark said. "How are we going to figure that out?"

"Testing of the members of the Priestess of the Dawn cult. They've all been taking it," Smith explained.

"For a short while," Mark added. "What if there are long-term side effects we don't know of? What of we use it on him and it backfires?"

Smith stopped what he was doing. "Mark, we have not decided to use it on *him*."

"But it's one option."

"It is." Smith pursed his lips sourly. "There may come a time when CURE needs a new enforcement arm. That time may come soon. Remo has threatened to leave CURE—or at least insist on terms for his next contract that CURE can't possibly commit to. When the time comes, CURE must either fold or carry on with a new hired assassin. Remo's replacement must be someone with extraordinary skills and, quite frankly, with a better understanding of the chain of command."

"I wish I believed that GUTX was going to give us that," Mark said.

"It might."

Or it might create a bigger problem than it solved, Mark thought. The phone rang on their computers, and the computer identified the caller as Master Chiun.

"Good Lord," Smith blurted. "The call is originating in the Yucatan. Master Chiun is supposed to be in Haiti."

"We've got full security up and running," Mark assured Smith. "Whoever it is, they won't get into your systems and they won't trace us."

Smith put the call on the speaker, and the unmistakable singsong voice of Master Chiun said, "Good evening, Emperor Smith. Good evening, Prince Howard. I would request another helicopter."

MARK PUT THE WHEELS in motion and a helicopter was on its way in minutes to the rendezvous with Master Chiun, who was in an isolated village on the Yucatan Peninsula.

"You would impugn the explanation were I to offer one," Chiun sniffed. "Therefore, I shall not."

"But why did you leave Haiti?" Smith demanded.

"I did not leave of my own free will. I was abducted."

"Did you even have time to find Remo?"

"I had time. But I did not find Remo."

Smith's patience was wearing thin. He disliked being kept in the dark. Chiun relented and explained. "I went to the forest of mangroves and approached the village of the Holy Mother, then she set her acolytes upon me. Unlike the one I destroyed at Piney Point, these were not so easily killed. There was one whose skin could not be penetrated by the sword—I misshaped his bones to make him a helpless cripple. I removed the eyes from one who could see through walls. Knowing there were two more acolytes unaccounted for, I approached the village with caution, and witnessed the nightfall ceremony conducted by the Priestess. It was not the final ceremony, only the common festival of flesh that she stages regularly for her flock. It was as you have heard, Emperor. The bones of a voodoo celebration without any of its true substance. These people don't know what they are truly worshipping. And they seem not to care."

"The entire village is likely influenced by

GUTX," Smith said. "In the food. Remember how the visitors to Union Island were drugged daily."

"I remember. Remo, too, has been poisoned with the substance."

"How do you know?"

"He left me a message, in the final moments of his free will. I witnessed the ceremony for many hours, eager to see Remo brought forth so that I might abscond with him, and I kept my presence hidden lest the last two acolytes came for me. But Remo was never brought, and the Holy Mother sensed my presence as the ceremony drew to a climax. She dispatched her acolyte with the *khecari* to destroy me."

Smith was puzzled. The timetable was not making sense to him, but he held his tongue.

"The *khecari* is immensely powerful. More so than I imagined. When he could not kill me, he brought me far from the Holy Mother, and then I fooled him and took him in a moment of his distraction. He would not die, but he is broken."

"The acolyte transported you from the island of Haiti to the Yucatan Peninsula," Smith said.

"This is what I have been explaining, Emperor."

"In an aircraft?"

"I was carried. Like a rag doll in the hands of a romping child."

"Over the ocean?"

"Like a stone skipping on the surface of a pond."

Smith tried to keep the disbelief out of his voice. The last thing he needed now was to further insult the already miffed Master of Sinanju Emeritus. And Chiun had gotten from Haiti to Mexico somehow.

"Your chopper is on its way, Master Chiun," Mark Howard reported. "You should know that we succeeded in intercepting a package bound for the Priestess."

Chiun said, "Intercepted?"

WHEN THE CALL was finished, Mark said, "It's almost beyond belief. It reminds me of the old fairy tales about Seven-League Boots. The hero would get them to help accomplish whatever task they had to accomplish to set everything right. Every step took them seven leagues."

"But those are folk tales, Mark," Smith said.

"So is the *khecari*. Hindu, not European, but still a folk tale."

"There has to be a better explanation."

35

REMO EMERGED FROM the stone mansion with the first light of morning and stumbled into the swamp. He was leaving his full plate of breakfast where it had been placed. His mind burned with a need for different food. Untainted food.

He found himself wading in the swamp water, and then he slipped his hand in the water and came up with a gasping silver-scaled fish the size of his leg. He was starving, and his mouth watered. He slit the belly and filleted the flesh with his fingernails, and devoured the white flesh raw.

He felt stronger, and his mind felt more clear, and it occurred to him that he should walk away from this place. But when he tried to turn his feet away from the village of the Priestess, they wouldn't move. He tried to walk, and he walked away from his freedom and back into the arms of the Holy Mother.

He made his way back into the hundred-year-old mansion and into the courtyard. There were a few mud-plastered revelers still sleeping in the grass and the smeared remains of a complicated symbol made of white powder-like chalk. There wasn't much left of it, but Remo forced his unclear mind to think on it. There were shapes in the chalk that he ought to recognize.

Why?

Why was he here?

Why was he kept here? Why were any of these people kept here?

Why to any of it?

The answer seemed as if it should be important.

There were a couple of freaks hanging around the place, huddled in a corner and staying silent. The little mouse of a man, whom Remo had once been afraid of for some reason, was nothing to be afraid of any longer. He was a gibbering idiot, picking crumbs from the mortar between the old stones of the wall as he crouched in the dirt. He was hit in the back of the head now and then by his companion, whose skin condition had become worse. His eyes were scabbed over, making him blind, and his limbs were crooked. When Remo came upon them, they were oblivious to his presence until he spoke.

"You guys party a little too hearty last night or what?"

The little mouse man flopped onto the dirt and shook violently. The one with the skin condition tried to stand, but his legs buckled on broken bones that appeared to give him a handful of extra knee joints, and he sat again.

"Did I do that?" Remo wondered out loud.

Neither of them answered. Remo couldn't remember. Looked like his handiwork.

When he returned to the chamber of the Priestess she was on her great low bed, wearing only the morning sun. Remo wanted her. It was an animal, physical want, and his breakfast had energized him enough to act upon his desires.

She awoke when he joined her in the bed, her eyes shrouded in sleep, but they became bright and eager and she opened up for him without a word.

Remo's mind was unable to work at its full capacity, but his instincts brought out the pleasure practices that were known to the Masters of Sinanju and he played Dawn Summens like some musical instrument until she sang her pleasure. Remo wasn't listening. He was interested only in satisfying his own body.

But there came a moment when a trickle of intellect penetrated the storm of lust.

"What are you doing? Don't stop now," she hissed.

He grimaced, and finished the act with a higher degree of self-control.

Dawn Summens slumped in her bed, wearing an exhausted smile. "My Remo. This is what I want from you."

"I know."

"You will give me your gift again."

"Yes, Priestess."

"Whenever I ask it of you."

"Yes, Priestess."

36

The special-ops pilot had seen a lot of weird things in his time. It was amazing what qualified as a VIP who rated special treatment—at huge taxpayer expense— by the U.S. military. He had transported undercover agents who looked like peasants and terrorists. He had lifted out dying men and rescued whole families who were in danger of imminent attack. Once, he had been called in to airlift a boy and his pet pig, only to realize the boy was actually a very small adult who had been undercover in a Bolivian terror cell. The pet pig—the special-ops pilot had never learned anything more about the pig. It looked like an ordinary, twenty-pound porker, but you just never knew.

But this was his strangest-looking human passenger so far. The man was Chinese or something, and he had to be eighty or ninety years old. His dress was a robe covered with hand embroidery, although it seemed a little worse for wear.

"Would you like some shoes, sir?" the pilot said when he went back to check on his passenger.

The passenger disdained the seats; he was cross-legged on the floor, meditating. He opened his eyes for the pilot and glared at the big, black boots he wore with his uniform.

"You do not, I take it, have a supply of sandals aboard?"

"No, sir. But we have emergency packs with adjustable combat shoes."

"I prefer to remain barefoot."

"Yes, sir."

Back in the cockpit, he reported his conversation to his copilot. "Can you believe it? He wants to get dropped off in Haiti with nothing. He wouldn't even take a change of clothes."

"So he's fashionable," the copilot joked.

"Huh?"

"You know. That robe. It's a Koh-Mo-No. They're really popular on the East Coast."

"Guess I'm not current on all the trends."

"It started in the kung fu clubs," the copilot said. "My nephew has one of them. Says it gets him girls."

"You gotta be kidding me. In my day, if a kid wore a pretty dress to school the girls wouldn't get anywhere near him and the boys would beat the crap outta him."

"Not my nephew," the copilot said. "He knows kung fu. Or crazy drunken karate or some sorta shit. Anyway, he can almost kick *my* ass. He wears whatever he wants and he's the coolest kid in school."

"Funny. I don't see our old friend in the back kicking anybody's ass ever."

The copilot agreed but said, "You never know about people."

AT LAST he was back on the soil of the island of Hispaniola, after his jarring journey and his humiliating plea for aid from the emperor. It had rankled him greatly to hear the disbelief in the voice of the emperor, who accepted nothing his computers could not process for him. Chiun would have searched for other transportation back to Haiti, but that would have taken some time, and Remo's fate hung in the balance.

Now, Chiun slipped through the mangroves again with all the caution he could muster, his senses tuned outward, stopping often to listen for signs of danger.

But the danger would not be heard. Maybe the danger would not even make itself known, until the moment it became too late. There was one acolyte remaining for him to face, and it would be the most dangerous of them all.

Chiun had extracted the full roster of his enemies from Sandal Wearer at Piney Point.

The hateful leader, called Leatherhead by the village people, had the power of *khadga,* so that his skin was impervious to the blade and even to the supersharp and strong Knives of Eternity, which Chiun carried on the tips of his fingers. But Leatherhead was not more powerful than the Master of Sinanju.

No force on earth matched the powers of Sinanju.

Jar Carrier, who used his *anjana* ointment of rendered fat on his eyes to see through solid things, to learn secrets and watch for enemies, was blinded. His eyes were destroyed with the burning fat of the *anjana* itself, and the ointment was burned up.

Sandal Wearer himself, with the sandals that allowed him to run forever at fantastic speed, was vanquished and his heart removed and burned.

The one that the villagers called Treetop Man had been the most formidable, with his power that was akin to flying—it allowed him to leap a hundred feet or more at fantastic speed. He had done the most damage by delaying Chiun's mission. Now Treetop Man was only another crippled, helpless creature stuck in a hole in the earth.

But there was one acolyte unaccounted for in Chiun's experience. It was the one the villagers laughingly called Drunkard. He had *parapura-*

praveshana, the power to enter the body of other men and see through their eyes and even control their bodies. This was a powerful acolyte, and Chiun was convinced it was this creature that had weakened Remo Williams long enough for his body to be forcefully drugged with the evil poison that allowed the Priestess to control his mind. Chiun dreaded his meeting with the *parapurapraveshana* because he didn't know how to fight the creature.

He knew but one weakness of this enemy. He could enter only the body of a male. He should never enter the body of a *sadhvika,* a female worshiper, or his power would instantly vanish and he would be trapped in the head of the woman forever.

Chiun saw no way he might exploit this weakness.

By the time he was back at the village, the afternoon was growing long shadows and the village was hushed. The people were talking in whispers. Worshipers were bringing armloads of wood to make a great pile in a weedy clearing in the rear of the Priestess's house. The tall vegetation was being trampled down by the people—it appeared they had not used this place for their ceremonies in any recent time. Tonight, the ceremony would be different. More momentous, to judge by the great bonfire being built.

Chiun's heart fell. He didn't know what events would occur, but he did know the purpose—to bring about the mating of the Holy Mother and the Destroyer of Worlds.

But where was Remo.

And where lurked the dangerous and powerful *parapurapraveshana*?

"WANT SOME?" Remo held up the glistening white flesh.

The ruined creatures huddled on the floor quavered at the sound of his voice.

"Mouse Man? I'm talking to you."

The *parapurapraveshana* mewled and tried to shrink into the stones.

"Want some fillet of fish, sweetheart?" Remo asked the Priestess on the bed.

"I want my Remo."

"Criminy. Again? I need to restore my energy. You've taken a lot out of me today."

"And you've put a lot into me."

"You know, sometimes I like it when girls talk dirty. You, not so much."

The crippled bones that were once called Leatherhead heard the words and wanted to scream, *Priestess, hear his insolence! His will is strong and returning! Heed the danger!* But Leatherhead's mouth was sealed in scar tissue. He could barely breathe through scabrous gaps where his nostrils had been. Speaking was out of the question.

So was eating, even though the aroma of the fish made him ravenous.

Remo ate the fish. It couldn't have been fresher—ninety seconds before it had been swimming in the swamp out back.

"Now. Come to me."

"Can't we take a breather?" Remo asked.

"Come to me!"

"Let me get rid of the rabble first. Why'd you let them in?"

"The sun pains their wounds. Ignore them."

"I can't do it with them just lying there."

"You will. Now. Come to my bed."

Remo went to her bed, and did as he was told, even with the crippled acolytes heaped in the corner and hearing all of it.

CHIUN THOUGHT. So much wood. Such a massive fire. Did it signal what he expected it to signal?

The clearing would become the *shmashana*—the cremation ground. Here many secrets were revealed. Their ritual cremation recreated the legendary cremation of the demons by Kali, and the ritual gave her strength on earth.

Ah, this was the reason for all of it. Now Chiun understood. Kali called her cult together to create a flock of humanity that would serve as the fuel of her return to earth. As the worshipers burned, they would release their life force in some way that would give strength to Kali, allowing the pathway to be opened. Then Kali would be free to come fully into the earthly world, to fully possess the body of the Priestess. Dawn Summens would then become the true avatar of the Holy Mother, and in that form she would mate with the avatar of Shiva and bring about Shiva Shakti. They would summon the dawn of a new world—and Remo/Shiva would bring about the end of this one.

Chiun could no longer afford to be cautious. The event was imminent. He must be bold—even at the risk of being overpowered by Drunkard. If that occurred, then he would be at best helpless, at worst dead.

But dead he would likely be if he did nothing.

Chiun came to the ground inside the village and trod barefoot upon the recent wooden walkways and the century-old stone paths until he came to the mansion of the Priestess. He walked with a rigid spine and sharp hazel eyes, and no one would have known from seeing him that the sharpness had returned to his body, like a long needle driven into his side.

He came through the courtyard, where the fountain ran crystal-clean, its constant flow having purged the mud of last night's ceremony. He entered through the double doors into the private courtyard beyond, where the sun shadows grew long and all was silent. But there was activity within.

Chiun opened the double doors and entered the private chamber.

37

The Priestess leaped from her bed and pulled the sheet around her.

"Now you choose to be modest, Priestess," said the Master of Sinanju Emeritus. "My son, come to my side."

Remo Williams looked around the room, his face alert and curious—and also confused.

"Why are you here, old man?"

"What have you done to my son?" Chiun asked.

"Blinded him to you," the Priestess snapped. "He does not see or hear you. When he tries to sense you, his mind is pulled in other directions."

Chiun pursed his lips. The pain in his side throbbed, but there was another pain in his heart. Was this true? Could she do such a thing? Remo was staring about the room as if searching for something and unable to find it.

Chiun was as nothing to Remo.

"What's going on? Who are you talking to?" Remo said.

"Hush!" the Priestess commanded.

Remo's lips shut.

"Get dressed," she added.

"Thank God."

"I said hush! Old man, you will leave my company."

"Without an escort?" Chiun asked as he went to examine the creatures lying in heaps on one side of the room.

There were, to Chiun's delight, three of them.

"Such violence," Chiun chided. "I see the *khadga.* I attended to him myself. And this is the one with the *anjana* ointment. I burned his eyes. For your enlightenment, I have met your *paduka siddhi.* I removed his heart and put it in a fire to burn."

"Leave this place," the Priestess said.

"The *khecari* I have also met. We took a journey together. It was an inconvenience. He is broken and stuffed in a hole."

"Get out!"

Remo said nothing, but he was bothered by the agitation of the Priestess.

"I am most delighted to see this one," Chiun said in his singsong voice. "The *parapurapraveshana.*" Chiun lifted the mousy, quivering man by the nape of the neck and shook him. "May I ask what became of him?"

The mousy man squeaked and trembled.

"I will assume he met with the mind of Remo Williams."

Remo gaped at the mousy man. He must have appeared to be levitating from the floor.

"I know how it can be," Chiun said to the *parapurapraveshana*. "Remo's mind is full of nonsense and misinformation. It works in inexplicable ways. Were I to find myself thrust into such a disheveled brain, I, too, would likely go insane."

Chiun dropped the man, who tried to crawl away.

"There is nothing you can do here," the Priestess said.

Chiun knew this to be true—but he tried anyway. He came to the Priestess like a slipping shadow to strike her down—and Remo was there. He moved with all his healthy speed and skill. Chiun had sought to spear the Priestess through the brain, but Remo sent Chiun flying back with a powerful Sinanju blow.

"That son of a bitch!" Remo blurted. "Where'd he go?"

"Be still!" the Priestess snapped.

"I thought he was all messed up!" Remo said. Then he walked over to the crippled body of Leatherhead and lifted it off the ground, just as Chiun had lifted Drunkard. Remo shook Leatherhead and tested the shattered limbs. "He is messed up. That was a different Leatherhead. Did you know there were two of them?"

Chiun crept out of the shadows and struck again, aiming a heart-bursting blow at the Priestess's chest, but Remo came between them and snatched at Chiun's arm. Chiun pulled away and struck again. Remo blocked and struck. Chiun blocked and feinted and struck, then fell back.

Not a blow had landed on the Priestess, or on Remo, or on Chiun.

"Damn. He's a lot better than the first Leatherhead," Remo said. "He's almost as good as a Master of Sinanju."

Chiun fumed in the shadows. "Almost as good, indeed!"

"You see you cannot reach me through my consort," the Priestess called. "Let us have our time together."

"And then?" Chiun asked.

"Tomorrow I will release him."

"Tomorrow your very mind and soul will be obliterated. Subverted to the will of Kali."

"You speak nonsense."

Chiun knew that his words were nonsense to her.

She was but vaguely aware of the influence of Kali. She didn't know her fate. The poor creature that was Dawn Summens was being used like a pretty little tool by the vastly powerful Holy Mother.

"Is he still here?" Remo demanded. "I can't see him."

"Stay by my side and keep your mouth shut," the Priestess said. "He may strike again at any time. You will protect me, above all other things!"

"Sure. Okay. But is he here?"

Chiun was there, and he stayed there as the Priestess dressed for the ceremony. Remo stayed with her, as well, and there was a strange balance of power in the room. Chiun sought for a moment of weakness or inattentiveness on Remo's part, but of course there was none. There was but one Master of Sinanju in the world more skilled and powerful than Chiun and it was Remo Williams, the Reigning Master. Remo's alertness was complete, even if his mind was held in sway by the priestess. Chiun would never get past him.

But did he need to?

He left the chamber ahead of the couple and waited for them to emerge. Remo came first through the door, and then Chiun bore down on him. He rained blows on Remo Williams. Remo returned blow for blow.

Neither of them connected. It was like lodestones, the competition of Master against Master. Remo and Chiun could engage in this competition for hours without either of them ever breaking through the other's defenses. No other being on earth could engage in such a perfectly matched competition.

No one.

Chiun saw it happen.

No one on earth.

Remo was getting the message. Even as he was battling an acolyte of the Priestess in his mind, he began to understand that it was something else he battled.

Chiun pulled back. He vanished from the vision of Remo Williams as he stood at rest with his hands in the sleeves of his robe.

The Priestess came out at last and glared at Chiun and said, "You waste all our time."

She went to the cremation ground, arm in arm with her consort.

38

The drumming commenced. The wood for the bonfire was piled as big as a house, and it took an hour for the flames to engulf it, but then the heat was so intense that it withered the nearby mangroves. A stone surface that had once been the foundation of a long-gone building served as the Priestess's stage.

Chiun stayed on the outskirts of the cremation grounds, and when the ritual commenced, he made a nuisance of himself.

The Priestess brought forth a gourd filled with liquid, while her worshipers came forward rolling empty wooden barrels. When ten barrels were lined up, the worshipers streamed to the nearby swamp with coconut shells and came back with them filled. In minutes, the barrels were filled to the brim. The Priestess came to add her own flavoring to the swamp water, and Chiun knew it contained the poison that would give her even stricter control of the minds of these people.

He must not allow it to happen. He loosened a chip of stone from the wall of her house and sent it flying at the gourd.

It was wasted effort. Remo snatched the stone out of the air and sent it flying back at Chiun. For a moment it was a game of deadly intensity, but a game nonetheless. Chiun knew he couldn't hurt Remo. Remo, he imagined, knew he couldn't hurt his rival—whoever that rival was.

Dawn Summens splashed her flavoring into each of the barrels, then a ritual team of worshipers came to stir the barrels with mangrove branches. Chiun slipped across the lawn and snatched up a barrel. Its weight was considerable—many times his own weight—and yet he brought it off the ground as if it were made of stiff paper, and he hurled it into the bonfire. The barrel burst and created a plume of steam and quenched a five-foot circle of black wood, but only for a moment. Chiun sent two more barrels hurtling into the fire. Remo was watching the barrels fly without seeing who was doing it—and the Priestess's instructions included protecting only her person. She ordered him to save the barrels, and Remo charged at Chiun, and again they engaged in hand-to-hand combat in which neither managed to touch the other.

"You don't need to listen to her, my son," Chiun said. "Heed my words. I am the Master who gave you the life and skills you have now. Don't you know my voice?"

Remo struck and parried, a smile etched hard on his face. He enjoyed the match, but he never heard a word from the mouth of his opponent.

"Kill him!" the Priestess commanded.

Remo fought well, but he made no headway against the old Korean—and in the meantime, Chiun sensed the worshipers streaming to the barrels to take their drink of the holy, poisoned waters of the Priestess. The people enjoyed the spectacle. It must have been a battle staged for their entertainment. Certainly it could not be a real battle, since neither of the warriors was actually striking the other.

Soon the worshipers were done with their communion taking. The Priestess called Remo back to her side. She was kneeling on the stage and making her symbols. It was a *veve* and a *kolam*. It was the personal signature of a goddess. Remo looked at it curiously. His eyes were bright with recognition.

"All my people—heed the commands of your Priestess," she called. "Tonight you will prove your dedication."

Chiun drifted to the barrels, where only the dregs remained, and bent over them. He inhaled, looked up and smiled.

"The Emperor has hamstrung the Priestess," he announced.

Dawn Summens didn't know what Chiun was talking about, but she didn't like the look on his face.

"They are not listening," Chiun said.

The little man was correct. The worshipers were babbling and laughing. It was like any other boisterous night of revelry.

"Silence! Hear me!"

The people quieted down.

"Obey your Priestess!"

The people waited.

"Go into the fire!"

One thousand worshipers weren't sure they had heard her right.

"It is the cremation and this is your purpose. Into the fire. Burn for me!"

The drums trailed off and the voices were stilled. The worshipers had been coached in love of village and loyalty to the Priestess, but now she was asking too much.

"Too many in the flock, too little poison stretched out too far," Chiun said. "They will heed your offer of hospitality but never your order to self-immolate."

The Priestess fell on her hands on the stage and suddenly her eyes became coal-red.

"You!"

Dawn Summens was gone.

"Back again!"

The body of the Priestess was in the hands of another being.

"Like a leech, you are!"

"Merely a Master of Sinanju, Goddess."

"Never is there *merely* a Master of Sinanju, and never has there been a grain of sand in a goddess's hand as unshakable as you!"

"High honor, for a mortal man, Kali."

"It is your hand that has shaped this one, this Remo, into a belligerent who thwarts my influence."

"No, Kali, not me. He was belligerent long before he was brought to me for training."

"Hush and be gone! Remo!" The Priestess reared back onto her feet and aimed her finger at Chiun. "There is the enemy. Slay him or I shall be slain."

Remo leaped into the battle with a new intensity, and again Chiun felt the creeping needle of pain in his side. He and Remo traded blows that would kill any man instantly, but Chiun's blows became weaker. Worse, Remo felt it. He knew his opponent's strength was fading. He had only to press on and he would be victorious.

Then the end came. Remo feinted. Chiun reacted, but not quickly enough. Remo connected powerfully against the chest of the frail little Korean man. Chiun flew off his feet and vanished into the flames of the bonfire.

But he danced on the wooden timbers and whirled in the lashing tongues of flame so quickly the fire never touched him, and when he slipped out of the flames on the opposite side, no one saw him except the revelers.

"Now, IT IS THE *shmashana,* my consort," the Priestess said hurriedly. "Make this the cremation ground. It is in your hands to give me the strength I need to come fully into this world. Blood and souls will feed me."

"Blood?"

"And souls."

"Your worshipers?"

"Slay them. Do it!"

Remo stepped off the stage.

"Hurry! Burn them! *Obey.*"

REMO FELT his body move. There was a place where he was struggling for control. There was a nugget of will that battled his waking mind. But the words of the Priestess could not be disobeyed.

Don't listen to her. You are not in her control. You did not consume all her poison. Fight her commands.

Remo Williams picked up a dancing man and woman and propelled them screaming into the fire.

Don't listen to her.

Two men were snatched up and placed in the flames.

It is not your wish to do this.

Another man, another woman, one after another. The people began to scream and run from the slaughter, but nearby the dancing and the drumming continued. Remo snatched at the running people and forced them into the flames.

"Remo, you are giving me strength," called the Priestess in a voice that was entirely unlike Dawn Summens's.

Don't obey.

His mind was a battlefield of wills and they all belonged to him, and he was hardly aware of the murders he committed. The fire belched ugly smoke and the smell was a horror. The drumming stopped at last. Burning victims staggered out of the flames before dying, and now the revelry was at an end. The worshipers retreated in panic, but among them walked the avatar of Shiva, snatching them off the ground and slinging them easily into the unquenchable fire. He heard the screams of torment. He heard the pop of their skulls when their brains boiled and their skulls burst apart.

"Yes, my love!"

Stop.

"I am strong on this earth again!"

Murder and waste.

The revelers had fled. "Come to me now, my love," the Priestess called. Remo returned to her, his victims forgotten.

"You want this body," she told him. "Your being is consumed with lust for this body."

The Priestess was disrobed, a vision of loveliness in the shimmering firelight. At her feet were the symbols Remo knew.

"Take this body," she commanded.

He would take his pleasure in that body.

But then he witnessed the arrival of a phantom. It was a translucent figure, small and old and quick, bringing a burning brand into the cremation ground. A long stick was the standard. Atop it, twigs were lashed together to make a trapezoid pierced by a single slash.

Like the *veve,* it was a symbol that Remo Williams knew. It was the symbol of him, of his house, of his people, of the House of Sinanju.

"Kill him."

Remo tore into the translucent figure of the standard bearer. What he thought he saw was uncertain. The specter, then Leatherhead, then a faceless enemy. The enemy was less strong than before, and Remo gave him a kick that sent him flying across the yard.

But was the enemy dead?

"It does not matter," the Priestess shrieked. "Take this body!"

Remo Williams took her on the stage, in the light of the fire, atop the ancient symbols.

"My love, at last," she hissed.

"My Priestess."

"My Shiva."

"Kali."

The female screamed in her pleasure. The male clenched her flesh and shuddered.

Then he rolled away from her and lay panting from the effort.

In the raging fire, the boiling brains exploded from a human skull.

"My love, it is done! I am made Shiva-Shakti."

"You played me for a fool. Where is Dawn Summens?"

Kali laughed. "Burned away. What care you, Shiva?"

He stood. "I am not Shiva. I am Remo. And my obedience was to Dawn Summens. Not you, Kali."

"Do not be petty, lover."

"I am not your lover. You are not Shiva-Shakti."

A singsong voice announced, "Only when she has the semen of Shiva, she is Shiva-Shakti."

"That's from the Niruttara Tantra," Remo said.

"You held it back from me!" Kali's voice rose.

"And I'm going to have the blues to prove it," Remo said. "But I'll live."

"There is still time!" Kali gasped. "I can hold on to this body. Shiva! Hear me! Come to me before it is too late." Kali grasped Remo by the shoulders and looked deeply into his deadly eyes. "Shiva, my love, take control of your avatar and fulfill your destiny."

"Sorry, sweetheart," Remo said. "I've been controlled long enough. Shiva ain't showing."

Kali snarled.

"Go back where you came from, Goddess," said the singsong voice from the diminutive figure at the end of the stage. "You shall one day achieve your goal. Now is simply not the age for it."

"But for you it would be," she raged, and galloped to Chiun like an attacking tiger. Talons exploded from the ends of her fingers, and she slashed at the frail little man.

But Chiun was a Master of Sinanju, and he struck the human host of the goddess Kali before she touched him, and the human host spun off the stage and landed in a heap. She leaped at the old man again and he struck her down, then stood straight, his back rigid, his hands relaxed in the sleeves of a battered robe.

Remo caught her by the neck.

"Not the flames. You would not put me into my own crematoria, lover?"

"I have to. If I leave this body alive, Dawn Summens might come back. She'd start bossing me around again."

The face softened, and smiled. "And here I am, Remo."

Remo lobbed her into the bonfire. The fire screeched and screamed and a dancing dervish of flame stumbled out of it. Remo snatched it off its feet and sent it back in. He heard the crackling of logs and the thing emerged yet again.

"Remo," cried the stricken voice of Dawn Summens. "Save—"

Remo stiffened.

The body slammed burning to the ground at his feet, and no more words came.

"Save who?" Remo demanded.

"Yourself," Chiun interjected.

"Good advice." He grabbed the Priestess bodily and sent her into the roaring fire.

She sat up, then fell back.

"I believe she really could have dug herself out of

the grave," Remo said. "That woman does not wanna die."

"It is no longer that woman. Dawn Summens is wiped away from the earth. Be certain of that."

Remo Williams turned to face Master Chiun. He could see the old Master perfectly. No more blind spot. No more Leatherhead delusions. "There was a moment when it looked like Dawn was coming back."

"Kali's trickery."

"I was pretty sure it was."

"My son?"

"Yes, Little Father?"

"I would ask a great favor of you."

"Anything, Chiun."

"Put on some pants."

"Yeah. Hold on." Remo kept watch on the melting figure in the flames.

"She is dead," Chiun said.

"Not yet, she's not."

Then they heard the muffled sound of a bursting skull.

"I think that ought to do it," Remo said.

39

Remo found the mangrove he was looking for.

Chiun sniffed distastefully. "You may fetch the phone alone."

Remo stepped up the mangrove branches as easily as if he were climbing the stairs at Folcroft.

"Can I borrow your phone again, Wildman?" he asked the corpse of Joey Wild. Remo had been afraid of this thing a couple of days ago. Now it was just another dead body.

He flipped the phone open and it started working all by itself. Connecting, it said. Then he heard ringing on the other end.

"I think I screwed it up," he said helplessly.

"Hello? Remo?" It was the voice of Mark Howard.

"Hi, Junior. How'd that happened?"

"The phone? I programmed it remotely to connect directly to CURE. Glad you're okay."

"I didn't say I was okay. But I'm okay."

"Chiun?"

"He's okay, too," Remo said, but then he second-guessed himself and snapped the phone shut.

"Chiun?"

"Yes?"

"Are you?"

"Am I what?"

"Okay?"

"Do I appear okay?" He snatched the skirt of his kimono. "I do not know if it can be repaired!"

"I don't care about the robe. I care about you. Are you okay or not? I knocked you around pretty good. Didn't I?"

"I allowed you to believe so. It was a method of distraction. Your mind is easily deluded."

"When I'm brainwashed with fish poison, you mean?"

"Your phone rings. It is impolite to let a phone ring unanswered."

Remo snapped the phone open. "I'm fine. Chiun's evading the issue. His kimono might be a loss. The body that belonged to Dawn Summens got raked over the coals. She's burned to a crisp."

"Remo," said Harold W. Smith, "you ingested an unknown dosage of guaneurotetrodotoxin synthesis."

"What?"

"You were poisoned. The chemical may have lingering effects."

"Tell the Emperor I have a regimen planned to clean the pollutants from your body," Chiun said.

"Lucky me, Chiun's got a puke-and-purge weekend getaway in the works."

"Perhaps a medical examination would also be advisable."

"It is not advisable," Chiun said.

"Forget it," Remo relayed. "Nice work swapping out the poison from Dawn's mailbox. It saved a lot of people."

"What is the mood in the village?"

"Not upbeat. When we left, the Haitian caterers were refusing to deliver tomorrow's buffets unless they had proof of payment. The whole village is going to go to the dogs in a day or two. But I wanted to ask about the poison you took from Dawn's mailbox."

"What about it?" Mark Howard asked.

"Where is it?"

"Isolated," Smith said. "It's a very dangerous substance."

"Damn straight. Too dangerous to be isolated. It should be destroyed."

"It's in a very safe place," Smith said.

"Bulldookey."

"You'll just have to trust me, Remo."

"Sure, I will. Where's Sarah?"

"Still on sick leave."

"Double bulldookey."

"What became of the Priestess's acolytes?" Smith asked, determined to change the subject.

"Gone," Remo said.

"Dead?"

"Who knows? They're just gone."

40

The woman in the private corridor of the military hospital was in her early twenties, but she looked barely old enough for her high-school prom. She had the bearing of an older woman, though.

Her long brown hair bobbed in a ponytail in a blue elastic band, and she wore a plain gray sweatshirt and trim jeans. She looked like a very cute kid.

She was working on an enclosed bio-chem isolation case. Inside the airtight compartment, her hands moved rubber actuators to open the sealed plastic layers to get at the powder.

Sarah Slate spooned a pinch of powder into a bottle of injectible saline solution, which was sealed and placed into a tiny decontamination chamber. The heat and UV lights blasted it, then the door opened.

She took the jar to the security door and keyed in her combination, then looked into the iris scanner. She was cleared and the door opened.

The man strapped on the table rolled his eyes and struggled against his straps. He screamed into the muzzle.

"Relax, Fore."

"What is it?" he said through teeth that were strapped shut.

"Guaneurotetrodotoxin."

"What'll it do to me?"

"Hopefully make your life easier. And mine."

"Lying bitch! It's dangerous! I can feel it."

Sarah Slate poked it into his arm. The prisoner gargled and struggled, but it didn't do him any good.

She watched sixty seconds go by on her watch.

"Now," she said "You feel much better."

"You know, I really *do* feel better."

"You will listen very closely to what I have to say."

"Yes. I sure will."

"And follow my instructions to the best of your ability."

The Foreman nodded. "Yes. I will. You can depend on me, Sarah."

SENSOR SWEEP

Four freighters, armed with missiles to be launched
from mobile systems at four unidentified targets,
have left port in South Africa. The payload is a lethal
chemical agent and the death toll is incalculable.
For Stony Man, it means the speed, skill, intelligence
and righteous fury of those who place a premium
on human life will be pushed to the limits in a
race to stop those who would see the innocent
burn in the fires of fanaticism.

STONY MAN®

*Available
August 2006
wherever you
buy books.*

James Axler
Outlanders®

LORDS OF THE DEEP
Outlanders #38

The turquoise utopia of the South Pacific belies the mammoth evil rising beneath the waves as Kane and his companions come to the aid of islanders under attack by a degenerate sea nation thriving within a massive dome on the ocean floor. Now the half-human inhabitants of Lemuria have become the violent henchmen of the one true lord of the deep, a creature whose tenacious grip on the stygian depths—and all sentient souls in his path—tightens with terrible power as he prepares to reclaim his world.

Available August 2006 wherever you buy books.

**Hidden in the secrets of antiquity,
lies the unimagined truth...**

Introducing

a brand-new line filled with mystery
and suspense, action and adventure,
and a fascinating look into history.

And it all begins with DESTINY.

In a sealed crypt in
France, where the
terrifying legend of
the beast of Gevaudan
begins to unravel,
Annja Creed discovers
a stunning artifact
that will seal her destiny.

*Available every other
month starting
July 2006, wherever
you buy books.*

GRA1